THE BEACH WEDDING

Married in Malibu, Book One

Lucy Kevin

THE BEACH WEDDING

Married in Malibu, Book #1
© 2016, Lucy Kevin

Follow Lucy on Twitter : www.twitter.com/lucykevin
Chat with Lucy on Facebook:
www.facebook.com/LucyKevinBooks
http://www.LucyKevin.com
lucykevinbooks@gmail.com
Sign up for Lucy's Newsletter:
http://eepurl.com/hUdKM

Liz Wilkinson has finally landed her dream job overseeing Married in Malibu, a new wedding venue for the Hollywood elite that promises perfect, paparazzi-free happily ever afters. She vows to do whatever it takes to put the new company on the map. Even if it means working with her ex-fiancé...and pretending to be in love with him again, too!

As a bestselling thriller writer, Jason Lomax writes plot twists for a living. But he never could have imagined needing his ex-fiancée's help to arrange a secret beach wedding for his famous niece. Nor did he ever expect to fall even more in love with Liz the second time around.

When their fake dates—and kisses—become breathlessly, wonderfully real, will Jason be able to convince Liz that neither of them is pretending anymore? And that the love they once felt for each other never actually went away...

Note from Lucy

Four years ago, I wrote and published the first book in my *Four Weddings and a Fiasco* series. Five books later, after all of the Rose Chalet happily ever afters had been told, I knew that I wouldn't be able to stay away from writing about weddings for long. Which is why I'm positively thrilled to be launching my *Married in Malibu* series and introducing new heroes and heroines for you to fall in love with.

I hope you love everyone at Married in Malibu as much as I already do! And please sign up for my New Release Newsletter at **http://www.LucyKevin.net/Newsletter** so that I can let you know when the next story in this fun and romantic new series is released.

Happy reading,
Lucy Kevin

CHAPTER ONE

The beachfront property of Married in Malibu felt like it was a million miles from downtown Los Angeles, even though it was only an hour away. The bright blue sky overhead seemed to stretch forever, while the ocean was calm, looking almost like glass.

The ocean was a lot calmer than Liz Wilkinson felt just then. The small former boutique hotel was the perfect spot for a wedding venue, and knowing she was going to be in charge of putting on exclusive celebrity weddings sent tingles of excitement through her. But she was also nervous because the owners, Rose and RJ Knight, had just arrived on site to take a look at the way things were shaping up for their new spin-off company. Rose, who was well known for putting on amazing weddings in San Francisco at the Rose Chalet, had decided to expand into Southern California, where the Hollywood elite would hopefully appreciate what they had to offer.

With Liz's honey-blond hair, bright blue eyes, and lightly tanned complexion, people occasionally mistook her for no more than the standard Malibu stereotype, as though she should be lying on the beach in a swimsuit all day long. So when it came to business, Liz always made sure that her hair was carefully styled, her makeup was elegant and understated, and her business suit was appropriate for the boardroom.

She'd been in more than a few boardrooms, as a matter of fact. Though she was only in her early thirties, over the past handful of years she'd put on high-level corporate events, conferences, and product launches for some of the biggest companies in the world. But she'd grown to hate corporate politics and the endless business travel—which was yet another reason that working at Married in Malibu was a dream come true. It felt like being part of a wonderful family business, rather than being just another cog in the wheel at a multinational corporation that assigned employees ID numbers to keep track of them. Running Married in Malibu was everything she had dreamed of as a teenager while waiting tables at a diner in middle-of-nowhere Kansas.

Now, as Liz led Rose and RJ through their newly acquired venue, she said, "As you can see, everything is coming along well for the opening next month. Of course, if you see anything that concerns you, please let me know and I'll make sure to take care of it immediately."

Rose's smile was both impressed and reassuring. "You're clearly doing a fabulous job, Liz.

Thanks again for taking the position. It's so nice to know our new wedding venue is in safe hands."

Liz had clicked with Rose right from their first interview, but even so, the idea of running a wedding business aimed at A-listers was thrilling—and daunting, too. Especially when weddings weren't something Liz had worked on before. Apart from her own, that is, which hadn't exactly gone well...

"We've kept most of the grounds as they are," Liz explained as she deliberately pushed her thoughts of the past away. "It's still a little overgrown, but we're working hard to get the gardens back into shape. It's great that you decided to keep the pool—it is going to be so lovely to decorate for receptions. We have also made sure that the access down to the cove is clear and easy for brides and their guests to manage in heels."

The beach cove had been one of the former hotel's big selling points when Liz had helped Rose and RJ find their new location. Married in Malibu had its own corner of sheltered beach, sealed off from the outside world—and it would be next to impossible for paparazzi in helicopters to get good shots of anyone in the cove. It was perfect for those couples who wanted to get married outside without any unwanted media attention.

"How far away do you estimate opening day to be?" RJ asked as they walked past painters' sheets and ladders.

"One month," Liz said. "Which is right on schedule, thankfully."

Rose smiled again, looking positively thrilled as she took in the site. "I can't wait to meet the new staff."

"Our team is an amazing group," Liz said, "and they're all very excited to be a part of what we're putting together. Everyone is waiting for us in the main hall."

Liz had personally headhunted her employees and was glad that Rose had allowed her to do so. It was one thing to jump in as the head of a team that someone else had put together. It was quite another to put together your own group of talented individuals, working out how they would fit together and what unique talents each would bring to the business. She was extremely proud that she'd been able to find such a highly skilled group for Married in Malibu.

The large hall was an arched, well-lit space with stunning views out over the ocean. Through the doorway she could see Daniel Brooker, the new Married in Malibu photographer, talking with Jenn Fairhurst, the cake designer. The massive form of the security chief, Travis Houston, eclipsed the more rangy build of Nate Waterson, the IT expert. Margaret Ashworth and Kate Bryson, Married in Malibu's stylist and garden designer, were having a quiet conversation in the corner.

The team—*her* team—all looked up as Liz, Rose, and RJ walked inside. "Hello, everyone. It's good to finally see you all together. I'd like to introduce you to Rose and RJ Knight, the owners of Married in Malibu. As this is the first time we have all been in a room together, and given that Rose and RJ haven't had a chance to meet you yet, why don't we do some quick introductions? I'll start. I'm Elizabeth Wilkinson, but please call me Liz. I previously put on events for large corporations, and I'm sure we can all agree that celebrity weddings are far more interesting than product launches."

They all laughed at that—a start toward breaking the ice.

When Liz smiled at Daniel, he immediately took her cue. "I'm Daniel Brooker. I worked as a photojournalist for many years, but I'm excited to be shifting gears into wedding photography. I have two great kids, Kayla and Adam, who mean the world to me."

Daniel was fair-haired, with a trim physique that suggested he ran or swam regularly, and was wearing a short-sleeved shirt, along with khaki cargo pants. Daniel had won plenty of awards for his work, and convincing him to come work for Married in Malibu had been one of Liz's major wins in the early weeks. She hadn't met his kids yet, but she hoped he would bring them by the venue sometime soon.

"Thank you, Daniel," Liz said. "Jenn, would you like to go next?"

Jenn was very pretty with dark, shoulder-length hair. She was smiling, but there was a hint of sadness lurking behind her eyes. She had clearly been baking already that day, judging by several small spots of flour on her dark, skinny jeans and navy blue top.

"I'm Jenn Fairhurst, and I've been baking for as long as I can remember. I'm really looking forward to having the chance to make great cakes and pastries for our weddings."

"I just ate one of her cupcakes," Daniel cut in, "and it was the best I've ever had."

Jenn blushed at the compliment and turned to Travis as if to silently ask him to take over the spotlight.

"I'm Travis Houston." He was easily the largest person in the room, built like a quarterback, his dark hair cut military short. In spite of the Malibu heat, he was wearing a suit, looking every inch a bodyguard to the rich and famous. But then, that's exactly what he had been before Liz had persuaded him to take a job with Married in Malibu.

"I'm the head of security," Travis explained, his voice deep and steady. "I will be making sure there are no intrusions from the press or the public while we're holding events."

Liz had no concerns whatsoever about his ability to do just that. "Thank you, Travis. Margaret?"

The woman who stepped forward was the youngest of their group, although her hair was carefully coiffed and there was a deeply ingrained elegance to her beauty. Yet, despite how perfectly put together she was, it was obvious that she didn't feel particularly comfortable speaking in front of a group. Fortunately, everyone was smiling at her encouragingly. Liz had heard endless raves about the parties Margaret had styled. Married in Malibu very much needed her on their team.

"My name is Margaret Ashworth, and I will be working as the wedding stylist." She was quiet for a moment before saying in a very serious voice, "I've been dreaming of doing something like this for so long. Thank you for the opportunity. I can't wait to get started. And I won't let any of you down."

Liz gave Margaret a warm smile to let her

know she didn't need to be nervous, before turning to Nate.

Their IT expert stepped forward, looking nothing like the standard image of a computer geek. Instead, he was tall and well built, handsome with dark hair that curled just slightly over his collar, and dressed more like a handyman than a computer specialist in jeans and well-worn work boots. Only the dark-framed glasses he wore hinted at the real nature of his job.

"I'm Nathan Waterson, but call me Nate. I'll be handling IT and our website, along with online promotions. But I want to let everyone know that if you need me to help out elsewhere, I'm more than happy to do whatever needs to be done."

Which left one person, a woman who kept glancing out the window, looking longingly at the gardens as if she'd much rather be there than in the middle of a meeting. Her long hair was plaited in a braid, and she wore a simple checked shirt and jeans. She was a beautiful woman, but seemed not to care at all about her looks.

"Kate?"

She turned back, slightly startled at the sound of her name. "I'm Kate Bryson, and I'll be growing and finding the flowers for the weddings, as well as taking care of the landscaping."

It was obvious that she was barely restraining herself from dashing out the door and back into the gardens to tend to her flowers, but Liz didn't mind. Kate's passion for what she did—and her amazing skill with flowers and gardens—was exactly why Liz had hired her.

Rose spoke next. "It's wonderful to meet all of you. I can't tell you how excited RJ and I are that Married in Malibu is finally coming together."

RJ smiled at his wife—with whom he was obviously deeply in love—before turning to the group. "When we decided to put on exclusive, intimate weddings for the Hollywood crowd, we dreamed of big things. But getting to work with a team like you far exceeds our expectations. We're both looking forward to seeing the magic you make happen here in Malibu."

Now that the introductions were over, Liz was ready to get down to business. Namely, convincing Hollywood to look at Married in Malibu as the place to get married.

"We will all get to know each other much better in the coming weeks and months," Liz said to the group, "and as we move forward, if there is anything you ever feel you need to discuss, please don't hesitate to pull me aside. Our opening date is a month away, and before that, we have a lot to do. Finishing the refurbishment of the venue and the gardens. Nailing our online presence. And doing our best to spread the word in every way we can." She took a breath. "Remember that, for most events, we will be restricted by nondisclosure agreements. That means not talking about the couples holding their weddings at Married in Malibu. We will be relying, instead, on our clients being so impressed by us that they're the ones who want to tell their friends and co-workers about using our services." When everyone nodded and smiled, she knew without a shadow of a doubt that she'd put together a great group. "Okay, then, let's get started."

Margaret headed off with her phone in hand, obviously ready to go through her extensive list of contacts. Kate went in the direction of the gardens. Jenn made a beeline for the kitchens. Daniel left to continue setting up the work room where he'd be developing both print and digital pictures. Travis said he wanted to check the perimeter fence. RJ joined in, too, saying he'd be happy to help Nate redo some wiring.

"I can see that you have everything set up extremely well," Rose said to Liz once it was just the two of them. "If you need any help, however, don't hesitate to call. And I can always get on a plane if you need me."

Liz had great respect for Rose. How many executives in the business world would have offered to fly out at a moment's notice to make sure everything was fine? The corporate world was all politics and machinations, not to mention the executives who made outrageous demands for conferences on impossible timetables. A world in which everyone else secretly hoped you would fail so they'd look better wasn't where Liz wanted to work anymore. This job at Married in Malibu was everything Liz had hoped and dreamed of since the days when she had been on her feet all day waiting tables, hoping for her big career break to come.

So if making the wedding venue a success meant working 'round the clock for a while, then it was just as well that Liz had absolutely no social life of her own, wasn't it?

* * *

One week later, Liz was impressed with how much the staff at Married in Malibu had managed to get done. She had expected that there would be a few start-up problems as they all settled into working together, but they were actually a little ahead of schedule.

Working here was so very different from her old life—in all the best ways. When she'd worked for major brands, her offices had always been blank, featureless, glass and steel spaces. She'd tried to bring some personality into them with inspirational pictures and personal photos, but none of it had really worked.

Her new office, by contrast, was a warm, yet classic space. Her desk, which had been sold along with the building, was a reproduction Louis XIV that had looked a bit over the top until she'd put a stack of bridal magazines and her computer on it. A comfortable, yet elegant sofa sat against the wall across from her desk, and she had hung a few pictures from her travels on the walls. It already felt as if it was her personal space, not just an office that she used during work hours.

Nate popped his head in. "I'm about to head out to Malibu T & Coffee. Do you want me to bring you anything?"

Nate, she'd quickly learned, was a bit of a caffeine addict. Fortunately, they'd lucked into a great coffee shop right across the street. "I'd love an Americana, thanks."

After he headed out on his coffee run, she turned her attention back to the notes on her desk that she planned to summarize in an email for Rose.

Kate had already ripped out the weeds in the flower beds and was preparing the soil for replanting. She'd been talking to a flower merchant when Liz had first arrived in the garden that morning and had been happy and animated, obviously well in her element.

Travis and Nate had been working all week setting up the security cameras, both to make sure that there was enough coverage of the grounds and to ensure that the camera feeds were secure. The last thing Married in Malibu needed was the risk of stolen footage.

"I still trust myself to take care of a security situation more than all these cameras and computers put together," Travis had muttered.

But Nate had shaken his head at that. "You can't be everywhere at once."

"Want to bet on it?"

Liz had been grinning as she'd left them to it. Next, she'd gone to check in with Jenn in the kitchen. Jenn had been baking test batches of multilayer wedding cakes, and Daniel had been photographing each as they came out.

"We're going to put up the best shots on the website," he had explained.

Liz couldn't help but smile at the fact that with a half-dozen different places at the venue where he could have started taking pictures, he'd chosen to begin in the kitchen with Jenn. Was Liz the only one who saw the sparks between the two of them?

She'd never considered the possibility of a workplace romance—especially when she was managing the staff members who were falling for each other. But it actually didn't bother her in the least. Not when Daniel and Jenn were both such good people, and she wanted nothing but the best for both of them.

A visit to Margaret had been last on Liz's agenda. Tucked away in an office that had once been one of the hotel's guest rooms, Margaret had covered most of the walls in pictures and luxurious scraps of fabric—an inspiration board taken to glorious extremes.

"How are you doing?" Liz had asked her.

"I'm fine," Margaret had quickly replied, as though worried about saying the wrong thing.

"You know you can come to me if you need anything, don't you?" When Margaret simply nodded but didn't say anything more, Liz continued, "I know how hard you're working to spread the word about Married in Malibu, Margaret."

"I've been telling my friends, and they've been telling their friends." Margaret shook her head, looking worried again. "I know that doesn't sound like much. I wish I had more to report."

"It sounds great," Liz assured her. Given how wealthy and well connected Margaret's family and social circle were, the names in her address book were exactly the kinds of clients the new business needed.

All in all, Liz thought as she finished typing up her notes for Rose, it had been a very good first week. Now she just needed to make sure they made the most of that start.

After sending the email to Rose, she was pleased to see that a few inquiries about the business were already starting to filter into her inbox. Liz didn't know whether it was the association with the Rose

Chalet, Margaret's word-of-mouth connections to LA's upper crust, or her own efforts at advertising the business, but people were definitely beginning to take note of their presence.

Still, what they really needed was an incredible wedding to launch Married in Malibu. If they could book a wedding for a Hollywood star who was willing to take a chance on a new business and entrust their big day to them, it would make all the difference in the world.

Liz spent a few minutes replying to the email inquiries, hoping that at least one of the possibilities would turn into an actual booking. In addition to sending out feelers, she had also been doing her best to keep up with all the latest celebrity news, noting the big-name engagements in the hopes that at least one would be the perfect fit for Married in Malibu.

"Who would have thought my job would ever include reading the celebrity gossip pages?" Liz murmured with a small laugh as she picked up exactly the kind of paparazzi-fueled magazine they would be trying to keep their clients' weddings out of.

Amber and Robert Plan Big French Château Wedding proclaimed the biggest headline, accompanied by a photo of starlet Amber Blakely and her fiancé, Robert Wakefield, standing together on a red carpet. The story suggested that the two had settled on a wedding in the south of France at a privately owned château.

If only Married in Malibu had been open a few months ago when Amber and Robert got engaged. Not only would theirs have been the perfect first wedding for Married in Malibu, but they might actually have had a chance of booking it, given that Liz and Amber had once been close.

More accurately, Liz had been close with Amber's uncle. As close as two people could be. Liz wasn't surprised to see a picture of Jason Lomax in the story about his niece's upcoming wedding. He was famous in his own right as a number one bestselling thriller writer, but she suspected the inclusion of the photo also had plenty to do with the fact that he was square-jawed, ruggedly good-looking, and in great shape despite a job that involved many hours sitting at a keyboard. People had joked more than once that his novels would sell even better if his photograph was on the cover.

"All of which means it's probably a good thing that Married in Malibu wasn't open when Amber and Robert got engaged," Liz said to herself. Because if there was one thing that made Liz's heart want to leap out of her chest, it was the thought of seeing Jason again. Especially after all this time.

A knock on her office door snapped Liz out of her reverie. "I'm coming," Liz said, getting up to let Nate in, figuring he must have his hands full of coffee cups for the whole team. "Hold on a second."

But when Liz made it to the door and pulled it open, she came face to face with a ghost.

There was no other way to put it. No other way to describe how it felt when Jason Lomax said, "Hello, Liz," as casually as if it had been ten hours since she'd last seen him rather than ten years.

CHAPTER TWO

Jason knew he was taking a risk coming to Married in Malibu today. A big risk with his own happiness and potentially his niece's, too. Yet Married in Malibu was also the best chance he could see of making sure that Amber did end up happy.

And he'd do anything to ensure that.

He'd taken Amber in when his sister had lost her battle with the bottle eight years ago. Jason had done his best to love his sister through all her problems, but it still destroyed him that Maxine hadn't been there for a daughter as wonderful as Amber. He'd been determined to give his niece everything she could ever want, even while he was still struggling to get his own dreams of writing thrillers off the ground. He'd had to learn as he went along, doing his best to be there for her through sometimes difficult high school and college years. Amber had turned out amazingly well, thank God. She was only twenty-three, but she already had a string of successful movie roles and was a rising star. Rising so fast, in fact, that her engagement to Robert was all over the press.

Jason couldn't have hoped for his niece to fall in love with a better guy. Robert was five years older than Amber and as steady as they came, working as a financial analyst rather than in the entertainment industry. Unfortunately, Amber had become so famous that organizing a wedding was no simple thing. Though they were still six months away from the wedding they were planning at the French château, news was plastered on the gossip sites every day. There was speculation over every little detail, from who was and wasn't going to be invited, to what designer Amber would be wearing, to the flavor and style of cake they would serve to their guests.

"It's all getting to be too much," Amber had told him when she'd checked in via Skype a couple of nights ago from the set of her latest movie in Prague. "If I'm not being asked a zillion questions by the château's wedding planners, then I'm being bombarded with questions about the wedding from the media. It's starting to feel like it's getting in the way of everything. My work and my relationship with Robert." Amber had sounded like she wanted to burst into tears. "I'm pretty sure a couple of the other actors on the set think that I'm nothing but a vacuous wannabe who's only interested in fame, but I swear I'm not trying to push my wedding into everyone's face. And neither is Robert, though even his financial clients are asking about it now. If I could just marry Robert tomorrow, I would. Even if it means going to

Vegas and getting married by some guy dressed like Elvis. I just don't want to lose Robert because everything has gotten so crazy."

Jason knew far too well how much it hurt when love went wrong. He also knew that it didn't matter how successfully things went in the rest of your life if it all felt empty when the person you loved was gone. In that moment that he'd heard Amber say, "I just don't want to lose Robert," he had vowed to do anything he needed to in order to help his niece with her wedding.

Absolutely anything.

"Don't get married by Elvis," Jason had said. "I'm going to work out something far better for you and Robert that will take all the stress off your shoulders."

"But you've got your writing. Your next novel—"

"Is not nearly as important as seeing you happy."

As soon as he'd signed off, Jason had put the draft of his current thriller aside to find a wedding venue that would be able to accommodate them as soon as Amber finished filming in the next few weeks—and that could also put on the wedding in total secrecy from the press.

The catch was that despite those constraints, Jason still wanted Amber to have the perfect wedding. She'd chosen the château because she wanted a magical day for her and Robert. The problem was that it had ceased to be about the two of them declaring their love for each other and had become a big media circus instead.

As Jason had made discreet—and anonymous—inquiries into boutique wedding venues with great reputations, the Rose Chalet in San Francisco had come up again and again. Unfortunately, the Northern California venue was too far away from Los Angeles for it to truly feel like home for Amber, and the logistics of setting everything up an eight-hour drive away would surely give the game away to the media. So when he'd heard that the Rose Chalet's owners were opening another wedding venue in Malibu, it had seemed almost too good to be true.

Especially when he found out that Liz Wilkinson was running it.

Ten years ago, Jason and Liz had been heading toward marriage and a life together. Until she'd broken up with him from out of the blue...then disappeared from his life entirely. For days, weeks, months afterward, he'd hoped that she'd change her mind and come back to him—or that she'd at least tell him why. But she didn't change her mind. And she didn't come back.

Jason had taken his heartbreak and channeled it into his writing. The heroes in his books all had strong undercurrents of darkness that never seemed to leave them even after they had conquered the worst the world had to offer. Critics and readers alike couldn't get enough of his dark protagonists, yet none of them had a clue where that bitterness had come from.

Losing Liz. That's where.

Now, standing face to face for the first time in ten years with the woman he'd once loved, it took absolutely every single ounce of self-control not to stare. His heart clenched at how incredibly beautiful she was. Even more beautiful than she'd been ten years ago.

But it was even harder to believe that she was in the business of making couples' dreams come true when she had shattered his so abruptly. She hadn't answered any of his phone calls all those years ago, and later, when he'd found some early notoriety with his books, she hadn't reached out to him then, either. If it weren't for his niece, he would never have put himself in the position of needing to ask for Liz's help. But he would do absolutely anything to make his niece happy.

Even face down his old demons...and pretend to make nice with his ex.

Before Liz could slam the door in his face, he stepped into her office at the exact moment she said, "What are you doing here?"

He'd figured seeing Liz again would bring up anger. Pain, too. But he hadn't been prepared for the powerful urge to drag her into his arms and hold her. He slid his hands into his pockets to make sure he didn't accidentally do just that as he said, in as easy a voice as he could muster, "I'm here to book a wedding."

The Married in Malibu buildings clearly weren't yet open for business, but that fit with the information he'd already gathered. The moment he'd arrived, his gut told him that the beachfront location with its sheltered sandy cove, the lush gardens, and a classic building that looked out over the ocean would be the perfect place for Amber's wedding.

Liz had paled slightly at his request to book a wedding, but recovered so quickly that Jason might not have noticed it if he hadn't known her so well. At least, he'd thought he'd known her until the night she'd walked out of his life.

"Congratulations," she said as she gestured for him to take a seat on the sofa across from her desk. Her tone was all business, but he could hear just the faintest tremor of emotion behind it. "When are you and your fiancée hoping to set the date?"

"I'm not the one getting married," Jason explained. "It's for Amber. You remember my niece?"

"Yes," she said in a far more relieved tone than she'd likely intended. "Of course I remember her."

Why, Jason suddenly found himself wondering, would Liz sound relieved that he wasn't getting married when she'd been the one to walk away from him ten years ago?

* * *

"That's lovely that you've come to Married in Malibu for Amber," Liz said, working to school her expression into a completely professional one. A nearly impossible task when her heart was racing faster than it ever had...and she was filled with such powerful longing for the man who had once been hers. "But I thought she already had plans to get married at a French château?"

Jason raised an eyebrow. "You read the gossip pages now?"

Just a few minutes ago, Liz had been wishing for a wedding as big as Amber and Robert's. It was true what they said: Be careful what you wish for.

If Jason had been just as surprised to see her as she'd been to see him, it might have been okay. No, that was a lie. It wouldn't have been okay, but it would still have been better than being the only one standing there in shock while he walked in like there was nothing wrong. That combination could mean only one thing: He'd known that she worked here before he showed up. Whereas she'd had no warning whatsoever.

Then again, she hadn't exactly given him any warning when she'd broken up with him, had she? If only there had been another way...

Forcing the painful memories away as best she could, she sat on the other end of the sofa, just one empty cushion serving as a buffer zone between them. "I'm in the wedding business," she replied in what she hoped was a steady-sounding voice. "Of course I'm going to hear about one of the biggest weddings of the year." Still working hard to get her brain to stop spinning from the shocking fact that Jason was right in front of her, she asked, "Is there a problem with the château? Because from what I've read, it sounds like a lovely spot for a wedding."

"That is precisely the problem—the whole world has been reading about her wedding." As his expression turned instantly protective, the deep way he obviously cared for his niece tugged at Liz's heartstrings. "Speculating about it. Making up stories that aren't true about Amber and her fiancé, Robert. Creating false guest lists, then saying she's snubbing other actors she's never even spoken to." Jason shook his head. "It's not what Amber wants anymore. Not now that it has become so big and important to the press. It's as if every new rumor is gold dust, and they're all prospectors fighting over who gets to lay claim to it first."

Jason clearly hated the paparazzi's intrusion into his niece's life. But then, why wouldn't he when Amber had always been as precious to him as if she were his own daughter? The last time Liz had seen her, she was a sweet girl barely in her teens. Slightly sad, too, given the problems Liz remembered with Amber's mother. Even so, Liz had been rocked to the core when she'd read in a magazine interview that Amber's mother had passed away eight years ago— and that Jason had taken her in. He had always been a good man. So good, and deserving of so much, that even though it had nearly killed Liz to break up with him, she'd truly believed setting him free had been the only way to make sure he fulfilled his dreams.

Again, it took a great deal of self-control to pull herself away from the painful memories as she said, "I'm sorry to hear that Amber and her fiancé have run into so many problems with their wedding. And I'm sorry about your sister's passing, too." Liz had been so close to contacting Jason when she'd read about the tragedy. Finally, she could tell him how sorry she was for his loss.

Pain flashed through Jason's eyes. "It was a hard time, but we got through it." Liz tried to convince herself that the silent echo of *without you* was just in her own head.

"So if Amber no longer wants a big wedding in France, what does she want?"

Jason didn't answer right away, as though he

wanted to get it all clear in his head first. She remembered how he'd always wanted to plot things in advance, as though he were writing the world around him before it happened. Sometimes it seemed like he'd had a full conversation in his head before he said a word. The problem with that, however, was when the story veered away from the outline...and nothing turned out the way you thought it would.

"There are three things she's looking for," Jason finally said. "First, with regard to the style of the wedding, Amber told me all they care about now is simply getting married and that it no longer matters where or how. But I know that's just her frustration talking. She deserves a special wedding day."

"Everyone does," Liz agreed. Although the truth was that there were plenty of people who wouldn't go to this much trouble for a niece—or even a daughter. Yet again, she felt that tug at the center of her chest at his sweetness. "Tell me your definition of *special*. I want to make sure I'm envisioning the wedding the same way you are."

Jason made a gesture as though he were trying to grasp the shape of something. Liz remembered that, too, the way he would move his hands in the air when he was trying to put words to an idea.

"If I had to guess," she ventured, "based on what I remember about Amber, I'd say simple but elegant. Beautiful, but not fussy."

"Exactly. Classic, but not tied down by too many old traditions."

He almost smiled at her then, and it hurt to watch him deliberately bank the urge. Because he obviously thought she'd *wanted* to break up with him ten years ago. It was what she'd needed him to think at the time, but nothing could have been further from the truth.

"One of the biggest problems with the current wedding plan is how complex everything has become. Not only with the pressure from the media, but also because the château has a thousand little details that they want to run by Amber and Robert, and it's gotten in the way of the work she's doing on her current film. Ideally, I'd want your staff to put the bulk of the details together without calling or texting her every thirty seconds with questions."

Liz couldn't imagine what it would be like trying to give her all to a role as an actress while simultaneously deciding every detail of a big wedding and fending off the press every time she walked outside. "Of course we could do that."

"Good." He looked slightly more relaxed now than he had when he'd first walked in—but not entirely at ease. How could either of them possibly feel that way with so much left unsaid between them? "I want their wedding to feel special because it's their big day, not because of the celebrities who are coming, or how much the wine costs. But at the same time, it's important that Amber's close friends are there, including the famous ones, and I do want them to have the very best."

"You're not asking for much, are you?" she murmured in a low voice. But then, that was what Married in Malibu was all about, wasn't it? To put on weddings for a high-end clientele with extremely demanding requirements. "Everyone here understands that while the peripheral details are extremely important, the fact that Amber and Robert are going to say vows of forever is the most important one of all."

Jason turned to look straight into her eyes. "You always understood what I was trying to say, Liz. Even when no one else did."

Her breath caught in her throat as she reeled from his sudden mention of the past. Especially because it was true that she had usually known what he was trying to say. In a lot of ways, she'd felt like she'd known him better than she knew herself. Until she discovered that he was giving up huge opportunities because of her. Walking away from him had been the hardest thing she'd ever done, but she'd truly believed it was the only way to make sure she didn't stand in the way of his success and happiness.

"I think it will really help that you know Amber," he added while she was still reeling.

"I haven't seen her in ten years," Liz said, not realizing until the words were out of her mouth that mentioning how long it had been since their breakup would open old wounds even further.

"True," he conceded in a voice that sounded suddenly raw with the same emotion she was feeling, "but you two were close back then. She even used to talk with you about boys, as I recall."

Amber had needed another woman to talk with about her budding feelings and obviously hadn't felt comfortable speaking with her own mother about them. "You know how much I liked Amber, but knowing her as a kid and knowing her as an adult are two different things. It's not like things just carry on where they left off."

"You're right, it's been a very long time." His

gaze continued to pierce her, and she barely held back a shiver. "Of course, you and Amber would need to connect again. She's in Prague, so we'd have to set it up over Skype."

Oh God...she could barely breathe sitting this close to him. Could barely keep from blurting out how sorry she was for ever hurting him, even if things had all worked out for him in the end, the very way she'd hoped.

Carefully rising from the couch on legs that felt far too shaky and moving behind the relative safety of her desk, she said, "There's no question that Married in Malibu can create a beautiful wedding for Amber." She couldn't throw away this chance when it was exactly the high-profile Hollywood wedding Married in Malibu so desperately needed. Not even if seeing Jason again made her feel as though she were splitting apart at the seams. "But you said there are three things you're looking for."

"The second one is simple. It has to be completely private."

"I've already spoken to our staff about the fact that they'll have to sign nondisclosure agreements for all of our weddings."

"They signed contracts at the château. It's not enough." He stood and started pacing her office, wall to wall then back again, clearly agitated on his niece's behalf. "The paparazzi still found out, and from there it's been picture after picture, story after story."

Thank God she had moved behind her desk. Otherwise, she wouldn't have been able to keep herself from putting her hands over his and telling him everything would work out fine. But how could she possibly say that when she wasn't sure about anything anymore?

Not since the moment he'd stunned her senseless by walking through her office door.

"Travis Houston, our security expert, has a tremendous amount of experience maintaining the privacy and safety of well-known people. What's more, the fact that Malibu is home for Amber means it won't attract the attention that her traveling anywhere else likely would."

"That all sounds good," Jason said. "But I still need you to promise that you and your staff will do whatever it takes to keep this wedding a secret."

"I'll do better than promise, Jason. I'll personally guarantee it." Even if it meant guarding the gates twenty-four seven herself. "Now, what's the third thing Amber needs?"

The way Jason looked at her told Liz he had saved the biggest request for last. "It has to be in two weeks."

"Two weeks?" Liz couldn't stop her eyebrows from shooting up. "We weren't planning to open for another three weeks at the very earliest."

"This is the perfect location for Amber's wedding," Jason reiterated, and she could see how determined he was to get her to say yes. Just as determined as he'd been ten years ago to marry her...

No. She couldn't think of that now. She needed to focus on Married in Malibu and the fact that Amber's wedding would be a great coup for Rose & RJ's new business. The best possible way to start, if they could pull it off. Yet the question remained whether they could. Nothing would be better for

Married in Malibu than a successful wedding for Amber. On the other side of the coin, nothing would be worse than failing.

"Two weeks is cutting it really, really close. I'll have to talk to my staff to see what they think."

"Don't say no just because of what happened in the past between us, Liz. This is for Amber, not for me."

Liz forced herself to take a deep breath before saying, in as calm a voice as she could manage, "Whether or not Married in Malibu agrees to put on this wedding will come down to whether we feel we're able to do it, and do it extraordinarily well, in such a short time frame. It won't have anything to do with the relationship you and I had in the past."

Of course she had to try to convince both of them that she could be utterly professional, no matter what. Yet, it sounded false even to her own ears. Maybe because there was so much that had lain unresolved between them for ten years.

Or maybe it was simply because after fifteen minutes with Jason, she could no longer deny the fact that everything she'd once felt for him—and had forced herself to give up—was now bubbling right back up to the surface.

CHAPTER THREE

Liz spent a few minutes working to clear her head after Jason left. But the truth was that no amount of deep breathing was going to make her feel any less like a bomb had just exploded inside of her.

She remembered the night they'd met as clearly as if it had only just happened. She'd been at a Hollywood party passing out pigs in blankets for a catering company, and when their eyes had met as he'd brushed her fingertips with his, their connection was instantaneous. Truly the most powerful thing she had ever felt in her life. More powerful than she'd even known things could be between a man and woman.

They'd fallen head over heels in love over the next few weeks. She would just look at him and be completely lost. As though there was no one else in the entire world but the two of them. As though nothing else mattered but being swept away in each other's arms.

But that hadn't been true, had it?

A bird chirping outside her window brought her back to the present. One where the only thing that could make matters worse was if she blew Married in Malibu's chance at a major wedding.

Pulling her shoulders back, she headed out of her office to discuss the wedding with her staff. She found Travis first, wiring up a security camera. "If we had a really great chance at a wedding in two weeks, do you think we could handle security for it?"

Liz actually found it comforting that he didn't say yes automatically. She wanted the truth from the people working for her, not just whatever they thought she wanted to hear.

"Yes," Travis said at last. "I'd have to coordinate with the client's and guests' security teams, and there are still a lot of holes to patch on site, but we could do it."

"Okay, then let's meet in the main hall in about ten minutes."

She went to find Kate next, who was clearing away weeds on one of the paths through the gardens. "Kate, if we were to book an important wedding here in two weeks, could you manage it?"

"We would have to use brought-in flowers for the displays," Kate said. "But that might have been the case anyway. I wouldn't say that we could hold the wedding out in the garden in two weeks, but if I used mostly annuals, I could make it look lush and beautiful through the windows."

"That would work well. They are talking about

an indoor wedding anyway."

"Who is?"

"I'll tell you inside in ten minutes."

Next, she found Nate and Daniel in Nate's office, making changes to photographs on the website. "An important client wants to hold a wedding in two weeks. I know it's a week earlier than we planned to open, but you two can do it, right?"

Nate started checking things off on his fingers. "In addition to getting the rest of the computer systems coordinated with security, there's the routing out to the cove so that we can get full wireless coverage, and a dozen small repair jobs to finish. But with enough coffee, anything is possible."

"I was hoping you would say that." She looked over to Daniel in silent question.

"I'm game for whatever we need to do, boss."

Liz asked them to meet her in the events hall, which left Jenn and Margaret. Jenn was taking a tray of bonbons out of the freezer when Liz arrived. "It looks like we have our first client, and the wedding needs to be in two weeks. Is that enough time?"

Jenn looked mildly shocked for a moment, but quickly recovered. "I'd need to discuss menus as soon as possible and find some wait staff…"

"Let me handle the wait staff," Liz said. "You just concentrate on the food. We're all meeting in the hall to discuss it."

Margaret was last. Liz found her in the room they were transforming into a bridal dressing area. "Can you come down to the hall to meet with the others?" She got right to the point. "We have a wedding. It's in two weeks."

"Two weeks? To plan so much?"

"You've planned parties quicker than that before, right? And this time it's not just you."

Margaret took a breath. "Yes, you're right. I'll be right there."

Liz stopped by her office, grabbing a stack of nondisclosure agreements. She headed down to the main hall, where the others had pulled a few chairs to the edge of the stage in order to use it as a table. Liz passed around the forms, and as she waited for them to sign, it gave her a moment to think about how important this wedding could be for Married in Malibu. She knew that this was the right thing to do, regardless of everything that had happened between her and Jason. She would just have to hold the reins on her self-control very tightly around him...even if she'd never had a lick of self-control while they were dating.

When they had all finished signing, she told them, "The wedding is for Amber Blakely and Robert Wakefield."

Their murmurs of surprise—and excitement— made it clear that they understood exactly what a big deal it was.

"Amber Blakely is huge," Jenn said.

"I thought she was getting married in France," Nate put in. When he got looks from the others, he added, "What? My job is being on the Internet all day, where Hollywood gossip comes to life."

"I think it's more the part where you're keeping up with it moment to moment that we're reacting to," Travis said with a smile.

"I didn't hear anything about them thinking of

changing their plans," Margaret interjected. The assumption that she would have heard wasn't at all arrogant when Margaret and her family were about as plugged into the LA social scene as it was possible to get.

Liz wanted to keep them all in the loop, but she also felt that she needed to be careful about how much to explain just yet. They were her team and she trusted them, but that didn't mean divulging every difficult detail of her past.

"Amber's uncle came to see me earlier. He explained that Amber feels her current wedding plans are getting out of control, so he's trying to put together a new wedding for her as quickly and locally as possible while keeping everything top secret. If you haven't heard anything, Margaret, it means that he's managed to keep it a secret so far."

"Isn't Amber's uncle famous in his own right?" Travis asked.

"Jason Lomax is a bestselling thriller writer," Liz confirmed.

"His books are great," both Daniel and Jenn said at the same time, then grinned at each other, more sparks flying between them.

"That could make it tricky," Travis said with a frown. "He might think that he's keeping a low profile by coming here to arrange everything for his niece, but his notoriety is still a potential security concern."

"I agree that we'll have to be careful," Liz said. "But before I formally agree to put on Amber and Robert's wedding, I want to confirm that you're all on board."

She was surprised by how much she wanted

this wedding to work. Not just because it was the perfect wedding to put Married in Malibu on the map or because it was Amber's wedding and Liz felt that if anyone could do it right for the girl she'd once been close to, they could. But also because she wanted to prove that she and Jason could work together without it being a problem. They were both adults. They'd both moved on. Even if there was still plenty of heat between them, she wanted to prove that they could do this. That she could do it.

When everyone nodded, she said, "Okay, then, I'll get all the specific details as soon as I can. For now, keep working on getting the place ready to open. I know two weeks is a lot to ask, but if anyone can pull this off, we can. And with style."

Liz headed to her office, already making a flurry of mental preparations. But before anything else, she needed to call Rose. And she needed to tell her boss everything.

Rose picked up immediately. "Hi, Liz. Everything going okay over there?"

Liz decided to start with the positive. "I have really exciting news—we're about to book Amber Blakely and Robert Wakefield's wedding! Her uncle came to see me this morning and asked us to arrange it for them two weeks from now. I just met with everyone on staff, and they all agree that we can pull it off."

"Wow. That's very impressive, Liz." Rose sounded like she could barely believe something so big had landed in Married in Malibu's lap so quickly. "How did they hear about us?"

Liz took a deep breath. "I know Amber's

uncle, Jason Lomax. And while I never thought my past would be an issue, with this particular wedding..."

"What is it?" Rose asked.

There was no easy way to put it, so Liz tried to give her the information as quickly as possible. Not the emotional details, just the facts. "Ten years ago, Jason and I were engaged to be married. We broke up—" No, she needed to fully disclose this part. "Actually, I left him a few weeks before our wedding, and I hadn't spoken to him since."

"That sounds pretty rough," Rose said in a sympathetic voice. "Do you think you will be okay putting on his niece's wedding?"

"Of course I do," Liz immediately said. "Honestly, I was just waiting for you to fire me when I told you about my past." She was only half joking. "I mean, given that I left my fiancé right before our wedding, I'm not exactly the best person to be going around planning other people's weddings, am I?"

"I'm not going to fire you," Rose assured her. "I'm sure you had good reasons for what you did." It was amazing how hearing that lifted such a huge weight off Liz's shoulders. "I am glad you told me, however, since I know firsthand how hard it can be to separate love and relationships from work." She laughed. "Just look at me and RJ—we worked together for years before we finally gave in to what we felt for each other."

It was good hearing Rose sound so relaxed about it all, because it made it easier to believe that everything might turn out okay.

"I'm sure everything will be fine between

Jason and me," Liz said again, more because she
didn't want Rose thinking that she couldn't cope than
because she was actually certain of it. "He really
wants to hold Amber's wedding at Married in Malibu,
and I know he'll do anything in his power to make
sure she has the perfect day."

"I think you're very brave to take this on when
working with an ex is likely going to be harder than
working with a stranger," Rose said in a gentle voice.
"I told you before that I can get on a plane anytime to
help out if you need me there. I'm serious, Liz. If this
gets to be too much for you, or if it's too difficult
dealing with such a complicated situation, give me a
call and I'll be there."

It was such a kind offer, but Liz wanted to
prove to Rose that she could handle anything that
came her way. She definitely couldn't go running to
her on their first wedding.

"I'll be fine," Liz said once more. "It's all a
long time in the past. I just wanted to let you know in
the interest of full disclosure."

After they said good-bye, Liz sat for a moment
holding her phone in her hand. There would be no
backing out now that she'd told Rose about it. Which
meant there was only one thing she could possibly do
next.

Liz punched a number into her phone. "Hi,
Jason, it's Liz."

"Do you have good news for me?"

"Yes. My team says that they can manage the
wedding in two weeks." Liz was doing her very best
to keep things completely professional, even though
just hearing him speak a handful of words made her

stomach flip. "I'll need to meet with you as soon as possible to go over the contracts and to figure out exactly what Amber would like."

"In that case," Jason said, "why don't you come straight over so that we can get started?"

CHAPTER FOUR

Jason's house was a gorgeous oceanfront contemporary on two levels, with large windows to catch the sun and blooming flowers everywhere. "I'm so glad you've decided to do this," he said as he led her through the house.

"It was a close call," Liz replied. Even though there was no denying what a big deal Amber's wedding was for the new wedding venue, a part of her still wanted him to know how difficult it was for her to see him again like this. "Fortunately, everyone at Married in Malibu is prepared to do whatever it takes to give Amber and Robert the perfect wedding day. Especially me."

Jason didn't reply, but from the intense look he gave her, she guessed he must be feeling the same way. "I have things set up in the kitchen. We'll Skype with Amber, and that way she can let you know everything she wants."

The house was expensively but simply furnished, its contemporary lines softened by several pieces of antique furniture. The kitchen was modern and sleek, a vision in white and chrome. But the table at the far end was far more rustic, a deep mahogany— where it could be seen between the sheaves of paper that covered it. There was a laptop there, too, along with an array of Post-It notes.

"You still like to work in the kitchen," Liz said softly. She remembered that he'd always wanted to be able to get coffee easily, or to be nearby while they were cooking something in a pot on the stove, simultaneously letting ideas simmer in his brain. The number of times a meal had burned because he'd hit on a great idea for a scene just as he was meant to be watching over it…

"Sitting here, looking out over the ocean, makes for a great place to come up with ideas and inspiration."

"I can believe that," Liz said. She'd always wanted a view like this. Her little garden cottage was wonderful, but this was the oceanfront place she'd always dreamed about.

Jason had clearly done very well for himself, just as Liz had hoped he would. When she'd broken up with him, his first book had been out with publishers and agents, trying to catch their attention in a world where so many others were trying to catch their attention, too. But Liz had read his manuscripts, and she'd known just how good he was. He'd deserved to succeed. And he had—spectacularly so.

"I've read all your books," Liz suddenly

needed him to know. They were dotted around the chaotic mess of her bookshelves at home, and she'd read most of them more than once. On dark, rainy nights, his books were always the ones that called to her. She could never resist delving into the magnificent worlds he'd created from his imagination.

"All of them?" He sounded...actually, Liz wasn't sure. Impressed? Surprised? Maybe even happy that she hadn't stopped reading his books just because they weren't together anymore? "There are quite a few of them now."

"I know," Liz said, unable to hold back her smile. "I'm running out of shelf space. They're good. Really good."

Jason's answering smile lit up the room, the first real smile he'd given her. One that made her knees go weak, just the way it always had. "I didn't think you were a big fan of thrillers."

"I'm not unless you're the one writing them." Her heart fluttered at the gorgeous picture Jason made against the backdrop of the ocean. "Of course I'm going to read your books."

"I simply try to write what I'm feeling."

She already knew that, because there was so much of him in everything he'd written. In the place of his heroes, regardless of their physical description, Liz always pictured Jason, his voice came through so clearly on every page.

She was acutely aware of how close they were standing. Close enough that she could have so easily reached out to touch him. Just one more step forward and she could be in his arms again with his mouth pressed against her—

Just then, Jason's computer signaled that a call was coming through. As Liz all but jumped back from him, she found that she could breathe more easily again. She hadn't realized she'd been holding her breath as she gazed at him and daydreamed of kissing him.

"That's Amber," Jason said, and while he was obviously happy to hear from his niece, there was a tiny hint of something else beneath his expression. Disappointment, maybe, that she hadn't actually stepped into his arms?

Jason gestured for Liz to take a seat while he arranged his computer so that the camera could view both of them. They had to sit so close that she caught the scent of his aftershave, woodsy and a little smoky, just the way she remembered.

Amber's face appeared on the screen. Jason's niece was incredibly beautiful, and it was easy to see the resemblance between them. The same jawline. The same intensity about the eyes. Currently, Amber's blond hair was tied back, and she was made up as if to go in front of the camera at any moment. Her expression was filled with anticipation and excitement.

"Amber," Jason said, "I'm glad you could meet with us today. I told you I would find a way to make your wedding work on short notice. You probably remember Liz. She's—"

"Liz?" Amber's expression froze. Liz was hit by the weight of Amber's stare—and her clear condemnation—coming through the computer screen. Turning her shocked gaze to Jason, his niece asked in an incredulous voice, "Uncle Jason, what's she doing there?"

"Amber." Jason's voice was gentle, coaxing. "Let me explain. Liz is the manager of Married in Malibu, the wedding venue I was telling you about."

"*She's* the manager?" Amber sounded as though she couldn't believe that the woman who had practically left her uncle at the altar could be running a wedding venue. Liz didn't blame her, since right then she was having a bit of a hard time believing it herself. "How can that possibly be?"

"Yes, Liz is the manager, and she's here to make things work for you and Robert," Jason explained, barely banked tension thrumming through his voice as he took in his niece's dismay. "She's your very best chance of having a beautiful wedding as soon as you finish filming in two weeks."

"I'm here to help," Liz said. "That's all. It's nothing more than a coincidence that I happen to manage Married in Malibu."

"A pretty big coincidence," Amber said with more than a little bite, but then she turned to her uncle again. "Are you sure about this? Are you sure you're okay with working with her?"

Beside Liz, Jason winced slightly at the way his niece had emphasized the word *her*. "I'm sure. I was the one who found Married in Malibu, after all. It's probably the only place that can put on a local wedding for you in two weeks. Fortunately, it's a venue that's been spun off from the very best in San Francisco, so I'm confident that it's our best option."

"Amber," Liz interjected, "I promise that I'm simply here to give you the best wedding possible in two weeks. Both myself and my team will do absolutely everything we can to give you a perfect day."

Amber hesitated for a long moment, before eventually sighing and nodding. "Okay," she said, although she was still frowning. "If you're okay with this, Uncle Jason, then I guess I'll try to be, too. It's just after the way she—"

"Working with Liz is going to be great," he assured his niece before she could finish her sentence.

Still not looking quite convinced, Amber said, "Okay, so now what?"

Liz made herself smile into the computer screen as she said, "I'd like to talk with you about what you want for your wedding."

"I'm not going to have to go through every detail again like for the French one, am I?" There was genuine discomfort in Amber's voice.

"No," Liz quickly assured her. "Not if you don't want to. But I do need some general details to get started. How many people do you plan to invite, for example?"

"I don't know," Amber said. "It's all gotten so out of hand. I mean, there are so many people who assume they will be coming…"

"Why don't we cut it back to the essentials?" Jason suggested. "Our family, Robert's family, and your closest friends. Thirty people. Forty, tops."

"I like that," Amber said, giving her uncle a small smile at last. "An intimate wedding would feel so much more like what Robert and I are really about."

"Great," Liz said. "Now, what about the color scheme and style? I know you don't want to go into all the fine detail—I have a great team that can work that out. But if you give me a general idea of what you might like, they will make sure to come up with something that fits."

"I want something classic. Simple but beautiful. But also unique. Has my uncle told you any of this already?"

"He has," Liz said, then verified the color scheme, making sure that Amber wanted the mixture of colors that Jason had suggested. She did. Just as she wanted the not-too-stuffy setting that he had put forward and an indoor wedding, as well. Jason clearly knew very well what his niece wanted, which meant Liz would be able to trust him to get the details right.

It also meant, however, that she would have to stay in close contact with him for the next two weeks.

"Your uncle has already told me how important privacy is for you," Liz said. "We'll do everything we can to keep your wedding a secret. We also have our own chief of security. Do you have security people he needs to talk to?"

"I hire bodyguards for events, and we have a security system at home, but I don't have anyone full time."

That was a little unusual in the world of an A-list celebrity, but not unheard of. Celebrities often wanted the minimum amount of intrusion into their lives, and bodyguards could be just as intrusive as the threats they were meant to prevent.

"All right, then. Obviously, the main thing is not to let anyone know what's happening. We'll keep things quiet at this end. I won't talk about the wedding to anyone but you, your uncle, and my staff. I promise that we'll do anything it takes to keep this secret."

"That's good," Amber said. She turned at a sound somewhere behind her. "Sorry, I have to go. I'm needed on set. I'll talk to you later, Uncle Jason."

"Talk to you later, sweetheart."

"And Liz—" Amber looked as if she could hardly believe she was saying the words. "Thanks for helping me with my wedding."

"You're very welcome," Liz said, and she truly meant it. Despite having become a big star, Amber was still a very nice person. And Liz could also see that she absolutely adored her uncle.

After Amber clicked her Skype screen closed and Jason and Liz were alone again, she said, "You two are still obviously very close. You really do know everything she wants for her wedding."

"We got even closer after her mother died and she moved in with me."

"I truly am sorry that you lost your sister and she lost her mother."

Jason closed his laptop carefully. "We all knew my sister had problems, but I didn't realize that she was that far gone. Not until it was too late." A muscle worked in his jaw. "Amber found her surrounded by empty bottles."

"Oh no." It was just about the most horrible scenario she could imagine.

"Amber and I kind of looked after one another for a while there after I was able to adopt her permanently. Turns out the teenage years aren't easy for anyone, but boy, did she turn out great."

Liz's heart melted at the way Jason had done so much to take care of his niece, rearranging his whole life to help her. She didn't just want to reach for him now, she wanted to wrap her arms around him, hold on tight, and never let him go.

But she couldn't. Not when that would only complicate things. And right now, both of them need to be one hundred percent focused on Amber's wedding.

Still, she needed him to know, "Amber is lucky to have you. Very lucky." She swallowed hard, then forced herself to return her focus to the wedding, rather than the way her heart was racing—and overflowing with longing—just from being in the same room with him. "If you have a little more time to spare, why don't we start going over the finer details? The sooner we get it done, the sooner my team will be able to get on with making this wedding perfect."

From the way he was looking at her—as though his heart was filled with just as much longing as hers—she thought he might be about to say something that had nothing whatsoever to do with the wedding. Something big. But he simply picked up a pad of paper and said, "Here's what I've got so far."

Forty-five minutes later, she had a file on her tablet covering flowers, menus, music, the order of the ceremony, transportation, and the bride's dress and measurements. With so little time before the wedding, having to constantly call or meet with Jason for additional details would only slow things down, not to mention risk compromising the secret nature of the occasion. And if that wasn't the whole reason she wanted to make sure that she got as much information as possible in this one trip, well, she was only human...and he was a very attractive man whom she now knew she'd never actually gotten over.

"I think that's everything for now," she said as she packed up her things and stood. And for a moment, she thought she might be about to get away with it.

"Liz," Jason said, stopping her before she could leave the kitchen, "that's not everything."

This time she knew for certain that he wasn't talking about the wedding anymore. Oh God...was he really going to do this? Especially after she'd nearly managed to make it all the way through this meeting without throwing herself into his arms? Without reaching out to find out whether his faint buzz of stubble felt as delicious against her fingertips as it always had? Without kissing him the way she was simply dying to?

Still, she had to at least try to head him off at the pass. "If we missed something with the lighting arrangements or the wedding party, maybe you could email it to me? I know I've already taken up time that you should be using for writing, so—"

"Why did you leave me, Liz? And why didn't you ever come back?"

CHAPTER FIVE

Liz knew there could be no more hiding from their past, no more pretending that this meeting had been purely business with no hint of personal feelings to intrude on it.

And the truth was that even if she had ended up deciding to hand things over to Rose and take herself out of the wedding entirely from here on—which she definitely wasn't going to do—Liz still couldn't escape the fact that she needed to finally give Jason an answer.

No matter how painful it was.

Forcing herself to look him in the eye, she said, "I left because I was holding you back."

"Holding me back?" He looked hugely confused, as if that was the last thing he'd expected her to say. "How could you possibly have held me back?"

"You have more talent than anyone I've ever met. You were right on the verge of breaking through as a novelist when we first started dating. But then, when we got so completely wrapped up in each other, you stopped going to writing conferences. Stopped trying to meet with agents and editors from publishing houses."

It had been so obvious that he would be a success. Once Liz had read his first manuscript, she'd known Jason had the potential to achieve everything he had ever wanted. And that there was nothing in life that could stop him.

Except her. Because while Jason should have been rocketing toward success, Liz was an anchor around his neck, dragging him back down. A waitress with a rough childhood from a small town who had moved to LA with big dreams? Everyone had heard that story so many times it had become a cliché. More than that, it had become a joke. There had been times when she'd come back from the diner with her feet hurting after a long day waiting tables, when even Liz had wondered whether she would ever have what it took to realize her own dreams.

"Wait a second," he said slowly, clearly working to wrap his head around what she was saying. "You left because you thought you were getting in the way of my career?"

"Remember that writers' conference in Montana? You'd always wanted to see Big Sky Country, but even more than that, you needed to see it since it was the setting for your novel. You suggested making a road trip out of it, said that we could have a grand adventure, see wide-open spaces, and make—"

Her breath caught in her throat. "Make love beneath the stars."

She could see him disappearing into the memory with her as he said, "You were afraid you'd lose your job waiting tables if you asked for time off."

She'd been afraid of so much back then— especially of how powerful her love for Jason was...and how powerful his was for her in return. "When I said I couldn't go, you said you wouldn't go, either. That you were happy staying right there with me, doing proofreading for the local newspaper, just as long as we were together." The old frustration bubbled up as she said, "But I knew you would never be content living in some little garden cottage forever. You were meant to be a big, famous writer, not to toil away in obscurity for a weekly paper with tiny circulation. You had so many dreams, such a sense of adventure. I didn't want to stifle that." She swallowed hard. "But you refused to leave me, even for one night. No matter what opportunities came your way, you always rejected them to stay home with me instead."

"I loved you, Liz. Of course I didn't want to leave you."

"I loved you, too. You know I did. But—" She'd never been able to say these words to him before, but with ten years of space between them, they were finally able to spill out. "You were so adamant about never doing anything or going anywhere without me that I started to feel like I couldn't breathe anymore. Like we weren't two individual people who were going to share our lives, but were rapidly fading into each other until I could no longer figure out who each of us was anymore."

"Why didn't you tell me I was suffocating you?" She could hear the pain beneath each word, and she hated that she was hurting him again.

"You weren't suffocating me," she countered softly. "I loved being with you just as much, Jason, to the exclusion of pretty much everything else. And that's what scared me. It frightened the heck out of me that suddenly both of us seemed to be letting go of the dreams that had been such a huge part of who we were up until we met one another. I wanted to talk to you about it, but you and I were never really very good at having serious discussions about things."

"Sure we were," he said. "We would stay up for hours talking about the house we were going to build on the coast one day—" A house very much like the one he now lived in, actually. "—and the family we wanted to have, and all the places we would explore together."

"You're right, we had no problem talking about the good things. But whenever I planned to talk with you about how worried I was that you weren't following your dreams—and my growing fears that I was on a dead-end path myself—you'd touch me, kiss me. And the next thing I knew I was so swept up in our passionate connection that I'd never actually bring up any of my worries. By the time we'd wake up in bed the next morning, I couldn't bear to ruin the moment. Not when it felt so good just to be with you."

"You still could have told me, could have found a time when we weren't tearing each other's clothes off to lay it all out for me."

"Even if I had, I still wouldn't have been able

to stay." She felt utterly bleak as she remembered the day she'd accidentally intercepted a phone call meant for Jason. "Why didn't you tell me the best writing program in the country had accepted you? And how could you have turned them down without talking to me about it? I only found out because they called the house line instead of your cell to beg you to reconsider."

He looked guilty for a moment, as if he still regretted keeping the information from her. "I knew how coming to California was your dream, and how much you loved it here. I couldn't ask you to go back to where you grew up."

"Graduates of that program have won Pulitzers and become international best sellers, Jason. It killed me to find out that you'd turned it down. And that's when I knew for sure that our relationship wasn't going to work. Two people in love are supposed to bring out the best in each other, but I didn't bring out the best in you. It was the exact opposite. Still...you have to know that it nearly killed me to pack up my things and leave."

He was silent as he processed everything she was saying. Finally, he asked, "But even if you thought you needed to leave for my own good, why did you do it like that? Without any warning. Without even telling me why."

"I know it was the coward's way out," she admitted softly, "but I also knew that if I tried explaining things to you, I would just end up in your arms, where you would persuade me to stay." Couldn't he see that it hadn't been about not loving him? It had been about loving him too much. "And then you would never have ended up going for your dreams and getting what you wanted in life."

"You keep talking about all of the things I wanted, but can't you see that the only thing I really wanted was you?"

The force of his statement took Liz aback. Yes, her feelings for him were roiling just barely beneath the surface. But she hadn't thought that he could possibly feel the same way ten years later.

"After you left, Liz, everything felt so wrong."

But she couldn't believe that, didn't want to think that she'd made the wrong decision when at the time it had felt like the only one possible. She gestured to the ocean just outside his windows, then to the bookshelf where Jason's books were lined up in their hardback editions, tangible reminders of everything he had already achieved. His career had taken off not long after they'd split up, his fame building, his name rising higher on the best-seller lists with each new book. She'd read interviews from around the world as he went on signing tours, traveling to all the exotic places she knew he'd always dreamed of seeing—Europe and Australia, Japan and South Africa.

"How could you say things felt wrong when you got everything you ever dreamed of?" As soon as Liz had gone, his success had followed, exactly as she'd known it would. She truly had been the only thing standing in Jason's way. "You've achieved everything you ever wanted. How can you argue with my leaving when it all worked out?"

"Are you kidding?" Jason demanded in a raw voice. "I was a wreck when you left. I was so broken up that I thought I'd never be able to put the pieces back together. I loved you more than anything, and you left without even letting me try to convince you to stay. If you had only talked to me, confronted me—"

"But you would have just held on tighter if I had told you I was scared!" The words burst from her lips before she knew they were coming. "Why couldn't you see how overwhelmed I was? I was only twenty-one. I came to Los Angeles expecting to work hard to achieve my dreams—but I never expected to find a love that eclipsed everything else. Why couldn't you let us each have a little space?"

He stared at her, clearly as stunned by her outburst as she was. And then, suddenly, a wave of sadness seemed to wash over him. "Because I was afraid that if I admitted that I was holding on too tight, and if I let you have some space, I'd lose you. You're right that I would have given up my writing for you." He shook his head. "If only I had known just how ironic our ending would be—that you'd end up leaving me anyway, all to save my writing career."

"Oh, Jason."

Her heart broke for the mistakes they'd both made. All she wanted was to find a way to chase away the shadows, and the pain, so that everything would be all right again. She wanted so badly just to feel his strength as she wrapped her arms around him and—

No. Liz clenched her hands tight, her nails digging into her palms hard enough that it hurt. She was getting caught up in him—in them—again. She needed to get some distance, or she wouldn't be able to think properly.

"I need to go."

"Don't go, Liz. Stay this time. Stay and keep talking with me about what happened between us ten years ago." He moved closer. "And about what's happening now."

"I can see that you have a book you need to get back to," she said as she stumbled back to put some space between them. "And I need to get everyone at Married in Malibu prepped on the details of the wedding."

"Liz, please—"

"There are only two weeks. There's a lot to take care of."

She scrambled through his house, out the front door, and into her car. Only when she was clear of the house could she breathe again. It had been way too intense in there.

She and Jason weren't like Rose and RJ, who were two halves of a whole and whose lives seemed to mesh so perfectly. Then again, hadn't Rose said something about how it hadn't always been smooth sailing for her and her husband?

"You shouldn't even be thinking about this," Liz told herself. "You have far too much work to do."

She had a wedding to plan, Jason had a book to write, and it wasn't like they were going to get back together or anything crazy like that. Not even if they'd been on the verge of a kiss in his kitchen before Amber had called and interrupted the moment.

No, nothing was going to happen between them. They weren't going to let their relationship derail both of their lives a second time.

She wouldn't let it.

CHAPTER SIX

Jason had always appreciated that whatever his mood, he could look out his windows and find some part of the ocean that would match it—some days felt like calm seas and others were closer to the rolling power of the waves. He often needed to stare out at the water for a while before he was ready to start writing for the day. Right then, though, it didn't seem to matter how long he stared out over the surf. He simply couldn't sum up everything he was feeling. Couldn't even begin to, actually.

He was supposed to be working on his latest thriller—the publisher's deadline was only a couple of weeks after Amber's wedding date. Early on, he'd learned that there was no substitute for simply sitting down and writing. He was currently working on a key chapter that would define who the hero of this novel was at his core, but Jason still wasn't sure if he had the guy completely clear in his head. After a fruitless half hour of doing little more than staring at the screen and seeing only Liz's face instead of any of the words on the page, he pushed his laptop away and moved to stand at the window.

If someone were to look up at the house from the beach, he knew how he would appear: brooding, stony, like one of the heroes in his books. But he wasn't unfeeling. If anything, he was feeling far too much. It was impossible not to when Liz had been close enough to touch and yet a million miles away. In the end, he hadn't been able to stop himself from asking why she'd left.

Her answers had left him reeling.

Jason's computer dinged, and when he realized that Amber was trying to get through to him on Skype again, he leaped to answer her call. Was she having second thoughts about the wedding at Married in Malibu?

"Amber, is everything all right? I thought you'd be busy shooting."

"I was, but I hurried back to my trailer as soon as I got a break. Is she still there?" Amber looked concerned. When he said no, she went on, "I need to make sure that you're absolutely okay with things."

"Don't worry about me, honey. You should just be concentrating on your movie and your fiancé right now."

"I know how much Liz meant to you. I know how broken up you were when she left. You don't have to pretend to be a tough guy with me."

"That was all a long time ago," he said, and though it was the truth, he now knew for sure that time hadn't done one single thing to diminish his feelings.

"It doesn't matter how long ago it happened. The point is that it hurt you. She hurt you. And now she's back. Are you certain that it's going to be okay working with her on the wedding?"

Thirty minutes ago, Jason would have agreed with Amber's assessment of things. He'd thought it was all so cut and dried—Liz had left and broken his heart, end of story.

But now he knew that their story was a million times more complicated and layered. And he was only just beginning to unravel his thoughts and emotions in the wake of all that Liz had finally explained to him.

Nonetheless, he wasn't going to let anything get in the way of his niece's big day. Not even the fact that seeing Liz again had spun his world completely off its axis. "Your wedding will be perfect, honey. Both Liz and I are going to make sure of it."

"I love you for wanting the best for me and Robert, but you know that's not what I asked," Amber pointed out with a slight frown. "I need to know that you're okay."

"I'm the uncle here," he said with a smile. "I'm the one who's supposed to be looking after you."

"I know. But I can't stand the thought of you getting hurt again."

For so long, he'd wanted to know why Liz had left. Now that he did, even though it was a lot to take in—especially the parts where Liz had pointed out that he'd been so afraid of losing her he'd held on too tight—Jason realized he actually did feel better.

Liz hadn't left because she hadn't loved him. Instead, she'd loved him so much that she'd tried to do whatever she could so that he could achieve his dreams.

"Liz and I have just spent some time talking things through," he told his niece.

"And?"

He smiled again, knowing he'd need to wrap his brain a lot more firmly around everything that had just happened before he could even begin to discuss it with Amber. All he could honestly say at this point was, "I'm glad she and I finally talked. In any case," he added before she could push again, "like I said, you don't need to worry about me, honey. But I'm glad you do."

They went back and forth for another couple of minutes about directors and scriptwriters and waiting around for an hour to get a shot that lasted only a few seconds. It was good to hear about everything going on in Amber's life—and to know how great it all was. Jason had always wanted to be there to help his niece build an incredible future. Of course, he'd never expected that Liz would factor into Amber's future— or his own, for that matter.

"Earth to Uncle Jason?"

"I'm still here," Jason assured her. "Tell me more about the tweaks you're making to get the script to work."

"No, we don't need to talk about that anymore. Not when I know you're thinking about something else. Someone else."

"How do you know I'm not thinking about my novel?"

"That's a different kind of preoccupied face." She looked over her shoulder. "They're calling me back to the set, but promise me that you will tell me right away if we need to look for another wedding venue."

"We're all set with Married in Malibu," Jason assured her. "You focus on your movie. Let me take care of everything else."

But Amber was right that he couldn't stop thinking about Liz. After being so close to her again—and finally talking about their past—it was impossible not to. Being alone in the same room with her was hard enough: She was so beautiful that he could barely keep his hands off her. But what she'd said had made it even harder.

"I left because I was holding you back" had shocked him. *"I never expected to find a love that eclipsed everything else"* had resonated deeply with him. But it was *"Why couldn't you let us each have a little space?"* that kept repeating over and over in his head.

When he'd first seen her again that morning in her office, Jason had been able to use the fact that Liz had left him like a shield to protect himself from what he felt, making it easier to keep his distance. It was never truly easy to stay away from Liz, but at least it had been possible.

But now?

Well...now he wasn't at all sure that keeping his distance was what he wanted. Not when everything he'd believed about their breakup had turned out to be so wrong.

Love hadn't died. On the contrary, it had bloomed so fast that it had taken over everything in its path.

Jason went back to the window and saw that the ocean looked calmer than it had a short while ago. Not pulling in so many different directions, simply moving with a steady power and weight that would sweep along anything that went out into it.

Just the way he had swept Liz along all those years ago.

Looking back, he could see now how young they'd been. He'd fallen so hard for her and had been so desperate to keep her that he'd told himself he didn't need anything but Liz to be happy. But he could no longer deny that Liz was right—he had needed to run free when he was in his twenties, needed to go out and live some of the lives that he wanted to write about. See places with his own eyes that up to that point had only been images on a computer screen and pictures in magazines. He'd needed to turn imagined settings into memories before he would ever be ready to settle down.

"She knew me better than I knew myself," he said to the empty room.

And the truth was that she always had.

The problem was that he hadn't known her well enough. Hadn't seen that he was suffocating her with his intensity, with his passion, with his love. He'd wanted so badly to be there for her, to prove to her that nothing was more important than their love, not even their individual dreams. But he could see now that if he and Liz had gotten married, they would both have ended up feeling completely smothered by their life together. Ten years ago, Jason had been barely more than a kid. He'd wanted to be there for Liz, for Amber, for his writing career, but he hadn't known how to do it all. He'd been stretched so tight emotionally that there were times when he had been afraid he would snap. He hadn't seen enough of the world, hadn't built up enough life experience to truly be ready to share it with anyone, not even Liz.

Just as she'd said today, love was supposed to make you better, stronger, fuller. But they'd both been too young, too immature, too lacking in confidence. Especially him. Which was why he'd clung too tightly. And she'd run.

Now, however, both of them were doing precisely what they wanted to do for a living. They were also older, full of hard-won life experience, and so much closer to living their dreams.

The only thing either of them lacked now was love.

Suddenly, everything clicked into place—both for his book and for himself. Because he finally realized that the protagonist of his book didn't need to be put through the wringer of any more dark moments. And neither did he. Instead, they both needed to risk everything for true love.

With only a few hours at his keyboard, Jason knew he could completely transform the life of his fictional hero. When it came to real life, however, he suspected wooing Liz was going to be a heck of a lot harder.

But he also knew that nothing would ever be as hard as living without her.

CHAPTER SEVEN

"I'm almost done setting up the sound system," Tyce Smith told Liz a few days later. "If you could put me in touch with the artist you've booked to play the first wedding, I'll tweak things to their specifications."

"I haven't booked anyone yet, but I'll let you know as soon as I have."

Liz could hardly believe that Tyce had set up their sound system. Even knowing that he'd started out working as the Rose Chalet's music director didn't take away from the fact that he was an increasingly big star. There were a dozen more important places he could have been, but he was clearly so loyal to Rose that he was willing to put those other opportunities aside.

Tyce wasn't the only person Rose had sent their way. RJ was helping to finish the renovations to the venue, which meant that Nathan had no excuse not to give his full focus to solidifying the framework for their computer system. Liz had already forwarded Amber's measurements to Anne Farleigh, the Rose Chalet's talented dressmaker, while Phoebe Davis was currently in the garden with Kate. Liz had half expected her gardener to resent the Rose Chalet florist's intrusion into her territory, but the two women were bonding over an azalea bush that needed careful management. In addition to being given assistance with setting up the music, lights, and floral arrangements, Married in Malibu would also be working with Julie and Andrew, the Rose Chalet's caterers, to help Jenn with the food for their first wedding.

"I could check in with some friends about their availability," Tyce offered. "And you could always get Rose to ask around. We know trying to put together your first wedding in two weeks while also getting the venue up and running is a lot to ask."

The Rose Chalet already had access to great people, so of course it made sense to use them. Even RJ's presence made sense—he might be one of the owners of the business, but he was also a tremendous help when it came to construction and renovation. But Rose was different. Liz didn't like the idea of having to call her boss in for help. It felt too much like asking to be rescued. Anything Rose could do for her, Liz should be able to do for herself, shouldn't she?

"Thank you," Liz said with a smile, "but I need to check in again with Jason to see if Amber and Robert already have a specific band in mind before we hire anyone else. I'll move it to the top of my list."

Ah yes, the list. Liz had thought she'd gotten so much from Jason when she'd been over to his house to see him. Yet it turned out that there were still so many holes, so many places where they needed more information.

The list had started out as notes on Liz's tablet, but she had transferred it over to pen and paper as it grew. She preferred a physical list, if only for the satisfaction that came when she was able to cross something off. Not that there were too many things crossed off so far, however.

After thanking Tyce again for all he'd done to help, Liz set off through the building to check in with the others. She found Margaret holed up in her office working on two big concept images that showed how the wedding could look. One was an Art Deco design with a jazz band and servers who looked like they had stepped out of a 1930s ballroom. The other design was much more modern—full of sleek lines, metal elements, and mirrors that bounced light around the venue.

"I like both of your ideas a lot."

"I do, too," Margaret said. "But..."

"You're having trouble deciding."

Margaret hesitated for a moment, then nodded. "Sorry. I know that you need the final layouts as soon as possible."

"Everything you're doing is great," Liz assured her. "But at this point, we should get a decision from the clients on which way they want to go. If you could finalize these designs today, I'll present them right away and get an answer."

"Great," Margaret said with clear relief. "I'll

put them in a file for you right now."

Liz headed over to Nathan's office and was pleased to actually find him there. Although judging by the sawdust on his clothes, he hadn't been sitting at his desk for long. Daniel was there, too, with one of his cameras connected to one of the computer's USB ports.

"I had an idea while hooking up the lighting with RJ," Nathan explained as soon as she walked in. "What if we were to project photo montages of the happy couple on screens around the venue before the ceremony starts?"

"I like it, but is that going to be easy to put in place in time?"

"We need to make sure our Wi-Fi is secure so that we're not accidentally broadcasting to the whole world. And get some great photos to project, of course. But Daniel thinks that if we take photographs as the bride, groom, and their guests come in, we could have them ready to go up by the time the ceremony starts."

"Obviously, those wouldn't be the final images," Daniel explained, "but it could add an interesting and unique element to the wedding."

Despite her reservations about the time crunch, Liz knew to trust her team. After all, that was why she had hired them. Because they were the best.

After telling them to carry on, she headed for the kitchen where Jenn was going through recipe books and making notes for the menu. She had smudges of flour on her cheeks, but on Jenn, that looked perfectly normal.

"I've got a couple of different menu options,"

she immediately offered, "and I think they'll work really well, but do you happen to know how many guests are vegetarian, gluten-free, or dairy-free?"

"No, but I'll find out right away." LA might be full of beautiful people, but they didn't stay that way without a lot of work. Celebrities could be the trickiest of all when it came to food, and no wedding venue serving such high-end clients could hope to get by without catering to the specific needs of every single guest.

Travis grabbed her on her way out of the kitchen. "After thinking things through more carefully these past few days, I'm going to need contact details for the guests' security teams so that I can brief them on our procedures. I'll also need to make it clear to everyone that on the day of the wedding, all security goes through me. That okay with you?"

"Absolutely, and I will get you that information as soon as possible."

She stepped out into the gardens, which had been transformed by Kate's efforts, with help from Phoebe. The tangled and overgrown sections had been replaced with lines of plants standing neatly in their pots, waiting to be transplanted into the flower beds.

"What do you need to know about the flowers for the wedding?" Liz asked.

"I was actually just about to come in to give you my list," Kate said. "It would help to know whether they simply want roses or something more exotic. And, of course, what we're going for with the designs inside. And if anyone has any allergies, because there are some blooms that are worse than others."

Ten items later, Liz had to admit that Kate was very thorough when it came to her job. By the time Liz went back to her office, her list of new questions was so long that she could easily have panicked. Fortunately, she had dealt with similarly overloaded situations in her corporate work and knew that the best way to move forward was to simply push her panic aside, put her head down, and tackle one item at a time.

Bothering Amber was out of the question. Liz couldn't add to the stress of her hectic filming schedule unless absolutely necessary. Especially not when these exact interruptions had been a big part of why she'd backed out of the wedding in France.

Which left only one person who could give her the information. Jason.

At his house, while she'd just barely escaped without kissing him, she hadn't been able to avoid delving into their past. In truth, were it not for the frenzied pace of her job here, she would have been able to think of little else but the way Jason had looked as he'd said, "I was a wreck when you left. I was so broken up that I thought I'd never be able to put the pieces back together. I loved you more than anything, and you left without even letting me try to convince you to stay."

"Just stick to the list, and you'll be fine," Liz told herself.

Even so, her heart rocketed around inside her chest as she called Jason, beating even faster when he picked up and agreed to come over in an hour. Just a handful of words from his lips—and knowing he was going to be close enough to touch again—threw her even further off her game.

Would he want to talk more about their past?

Or, even more terrifying, had he been serious when he'd said he wanted to talk about the sparks flying between them now?

* * *

By the time Jason walked into her office fifty-five minutes later, Liz's entire body was thrumming with anticipation. And memories. Memories so strong that one look at his bristly chin was enough for her to guess, "You've been working hard, haven't you?"

"I finished my book fifteen minutes ago," he said with a smile. "Once I worked out what my hero wanted, it was easier than I thought it would be."

"Congratulations." Liz couldn't imagine writing not just one book, but a dozen, as he had over the years. "Is this the final manuscript or still a rough draft?"

"I'll start revising it after the wedding." He sat down on the sofa, and he looked so good that she was grateful for the small barrier of the desk between them as he said, "Some things need time to settle so that you can look at them properly and really understand how to move forward."

She was almost painfully aware of the sparks flying between them...and of the fact that he seemed not only to be talking about his book, but also about the two of them. Or maybe it was just that being this close to him again was making her a little crazy. Because by *moving forward*, he couldn't possibly mean them, could he? No, surely he was just talking about his book.

"Thanks for coming so quickly. I'm desperate for more detailed information." She hid her discomfort over her deeply emotional thoughts by getting out the design folders Margaret had prepared for her. "First, we need a final decision on the theme and color scheme."

Jason took his time studying the two options before pointing to the arrangement with the Art Deco touches and the warmer colors. "Amber is looking for something classic, but at the same time she doesn't want it to feel like the same wedding everyone else has. I think it will be just right for her."

Yet again, Liz was thankful that Jason knew his niece well enough to make these decisions. He'd obviously built an incredible relationship with Amber in the wake of her mother's death. Not everyone could have managed that; in fact, a lot of men would have run from it. But not Jason.

Jason wasn't the kind of man who ran.

"Thanks for the quick decision. Knowing which way we want to go will make a lot of things easier."

"That's true of a lot of things, isn't it?"

"Yes, well…" Liz had a feeling he was talking about the two of them again, so she desperately tried to keep the conversation on track. "We will pick the flowers to match the room design, but do you know if Amber has any strong preferences? A particular flower that she's always loved?"

"If you can find something that manages to bloom beautifully in difficult conditions, that would be a nice touch."

Trust Jason to look for the meaning in everything, even flower arrangements. "I'm sure Kate can come up with something amazing. Now, about the guests, do you know who will need their own security people, whether there are any allergies or other specific requirements for the food, and which guests will need us to arrange transportation from the airport or somewhere else?"

When Jason smiled before answering, she had a feeling that he was deliberately trying to put her at ease. Clearly, she was looking far too stressed out. "I believe Amber's friend Hannah will have security with her, and possibly her current co-star, as well. I have contact information for both of them on my phone. Why don't we give them a ring now and work everything out?"

Thirty minutes later, when the security issues had been taken care of, they went carefully through the guest list. Despite how nervous being this close to Jason still made her, Liz couldn't help but be charmed by the way each name on the list came with a small anecdote or observation that brought it to life.

"Robert's Aunt Petunia has decided to backpack all over the world," he told her with a grin, "even though she's seventy-three years old. She'll probably complain that the food isn't spicy enough, but if you made it the way she likes it, no one else would be able to eat it."

"That isn't a problem," Liz said, already looking forward to meeting Robert's aunt. "I'll just get Jenn to make sure that her food is a lot hotter than everyone else's."

Liz loved the way Jason turned the people

around him into stories. People she had never met became living, breathing individuals to her, simply because he was describing them so well.

Although it suddenly made her wonder, how did he describe her to other people? And what story did he tell? Was it a story of the time they'd spent together when things were good? Or was it a story about the way they'd split up?

Working hard to corral her focus, she said, "Nathan, our IT specialist, has an interesting idea of projecting photos of Amber and Robert and their guests around various points in the room. If you agree that's a good idea, we'd like a few personal photographs to work with in addition to the shots we'll take when everyone arrives, so that we can have those available at the venue shortly afterward."

Jason thought about it. "It does sound interesting, certainly unique, but will it be secure? I know you would never give any of the photographs away or try to sell them to the press, but people are so good at stealing things online. Besides, I've never met a photographer who didn't want to play with their pictures forever."

"If you deliver the photos to us on a USB stick, we'll store them in that form, and we won't put them anywhere there could be outside access. And obviously, the photographs would just be early versions," she explained. "But if anyone can take great pictures without needing to retouch them, it's Daniel. I'm very lucky to have such a great team to work with."

"I doubt luck had anything to do with it. I bet you went out and hunted down the people you really wanted, the best ones for the job. I know you, Liz. You don't give up when you have your mind set on something."

Only, she had given up, hadn't she? The one time it really mattered...

"Thanks for agreeing to do this," he said in a deep voice that set fire to her insides. "I know it's a ton of work to get everything ready in time."

Maybe she should have downplayed how much work it was, but with everything going topsy-turvy inside of her—from being in the same room with him, from thinking about the past, from going around and around inside her head with all the mistakes she'd made and how she wished she could have done things differently—she found herself saying, "The trouble is that there are so many different jobs popping up from moment to moment. I truly do have the best people on task, but even so, I'm wondering if we simply don't have enough pairs of hands."

"I can help."

Liz froze. "No, I can't ask you to help. I mean, you have your writing to take care of, and—"

"Like I said, the first draft of my book is done, and I don't want to edit it right away because I need to let it settle for a while. Besides, right now, there's nothing more important to me than making sure that Amber gets the perfect wedding."

Okay, so maybe Jason did have the time, but that didn't mean it was a good idea. "I know you want her wedding to be perfect—and I do, too—but it wouldn't feel right for you to work with us when you're paying us to do the work."

"There must be something I can help out with—errands, manual labor, whatever you need. Come on, Liz. You just said you could do with some more help, with an extra pair of hands."

She did need the extra pair of hands. But even more striking was that a man this successful, this wealthy, this famous, would actually offer to do menial errands and manual labor. She'd fallen in love with him for so many reasons, and again and again, she could see that those reasons hadn't been wrong.

"All right," she said. "Thank you. We could use the help." She tried to make her response sound friendly, but not too friendly. Professional, but not cold. "I'll get back to you soon with a list."

She expected him to get up and leave then, but instead he continued to gaze at her. She could see his mind working...and what she saw in his eyes scared her. Scared her enough that she couldn't figure out how to head him off at the pass. Couldn't manage to get her feet to move her out the door, either.

"Thank you for telling me why you left, Liz." She could hear the emotion in his voice, the same emotion she'd been trying unsuccessfully to tamp down ever since she'd left his house days ago. "It wasn't easy to hear some of what you had to say, but you were right. I wasn't ready to be with you then. We were just kids. I tried to convince myself that I didn't need adventure, that I didn't need to see the world. But I did. I wasn't ready then—" She'd never seen him look more serious. "But I am now."

Liz felt her mouth fall open. Had he really just told her that she'd been right to leave?

And...oh my God...had he also just said that he

was ready to be with her now?

"Don't do this, Jason," she finally managed to reply, her voice barely above a whisper from the shock of it all. "We're here to support Amber and her fiancé. We need to focus on that. Let's put together an incredible wedding for her, and then—"

"Go our separate ways again?"

Liz forced herself to nod. It was really hard, but she managed it somehow.

But Jason was already shaking his head. "No, I don't want to do that—and I don't think you do, either. Can't you feel the heat, the electricity, the emotion between us?"

Of course she could, but she couldn't admit that to him. Could she?

"Heat? Electricity? They weren't enough to keep us together once," she pointed out. "If it didn't work before, what makes you think the second time would work any better?"

"Because we aren't kids anymore. I can see that we've both changed a lot since those early days, but one thing hasn't changed at all—how I feel about you. If we don't at least try, then how will we know? And I promise, if you agree to try again with me, I'll make sure I don't overwhelm you."

Liz had never been good at lying to herself, so she couldn't possibly lie to Jason right now and tell him that she wasn't feeling all the things he'd just said—the heat, the electricity, and the emotion. But at the same time she couldn't see that it was a good idea to just give in to it all so easily. Not when she knew firsthand how quickly everything could get sucked into the vortex of their relationship—with every plan, every bit of focus, being swept away before she even realized it was happening.

Somehow she needed to let him know it was all too much. Too fast. Because even though he'd promised not to overwhelm her again, couldn't he see that he already had?

She felt so topsy-turvy inside, in fact, that the only words she could get out were, "We need to focus on Amber's wedding."

For a long moment, he remained silent. Finally, he nodded and said, "You're right, again. Amber's wedding is the most important thing of all right now."

But even though he'd just agreed with her about their priorities for the next ten days, something told her he wasn't going to make any similar promises about his intentions after the wedding...

CHAPTER EIGHT

He'd shocked her. Jason understood that it would take Liz time to process what he'd said about the two of them trying again. Time for her to realize how good they could be together—a million times better than they'd been before.

So even though he wished he could find some way to convince her right there and then that they should be together again, as she walked him out to the parking lot, he forced himself to stay quiet and give her room to think. He definitely didn't want to make the mistake again of suffocating her with his love.

Unfortunately, as soon as they stepped outside, he saw a camera flash. It was instinct to turn around to look directly at the flash, which unfortunately gave the photographer a better shot. The young woman holding the camera was wearing jeans and a denim jacket, her hair cut spiky short. As she leaned against a motorcycle to get more shots, he was tempted to run toward her to grab the camera, but he knew she would probably just leap on her bike and ride away before he could get close.

"Damn it," Liz said beside him. "Travis was supposed to stop things like this from happening."

Sure enough, Liz's big security chief came stalking around the side of the building. He expected the woman to run. Instead, she walked forward with a cocky gait.

"Laurel Kingston, *LA Fame Scene* blog," she said. "I thought that was you, Jason Lomax. Are you here about your niece's wedding?"

"Miss Kingston," Travis said in a stern voice before Jason could reply. "You're trespassing on private property. I'm going to have to ask you to leave and to please hand over your camera."

"Touch my camera, and I'll sue you. Hey!" She yelped as Travis grabbed the camera and quickly deleted the pictures. "You can't do that!"

"As I said, you're trespassing." He handed the camera back to her.

"You still can't do that, and you can't dodge the question," she said as she pointed at Jason. "Are you here about Amber's wedding? You might as well just answer me, because otherwise I'll... Hey! Get your hands off me!"

Travis hadn't actually touched the woman, but he was good enough at his job to maneuver the reporter back toward her motorcycle just from the sheer scale of his presence.

Unfortunately, even without the pictures, the damage was already done. Just the fact that the blogger had spotted Jason at Married in Malibu would be enough to start rumors flying. There would soon be hosts of photographers trying to find proof that Amber was having her wedding there instead of at the château.

If Jason were writing this, someone might just "disappear." But this was real life…which meant Jason needed a better idea.

In a flash, it came to him.

He reached out and took Liz's hand, pulled her in close and pressed a kiss to her forehead. "Don't worry about her, baby. Everything's going to be fine."

Both Liz and the reporter looked confused for a moment, but the reporter recovered first. She got on her bike, then said, "You haven't heard the last of me. I'm going to find out what's going on here." She shoved on her helmet, then sped off, but Jason held on to Liz's hand as long as she would let him.

For a moment, it felt as if Liz were enjoying being in his arms, but too soon, she pulled back from his grip and said, "What was that? What did you just do?" She didn't give him a chance to answer before she turned to Travis. "And how did she get in? We're supposed to be keeping the press out, no matter what."

"We will," Travis replied. "We're just not quite set up yet."

Jason could see that she was frustrated, even a little bit angry, but instead of blowing up at Travis, she simply said, "Please hurry."

"I'll get right on it," Travis assured her. He hurried inside, and it was strange to see such a big man moving so fast. Clearly, he understood just how delicate the situation could be.

Lord knew Jason certainly understood it when Liz turned back to him. "You still haven't told me why you grabbed my hand and why you... You kissed my forehead!"

"It was for the reporter. To throw her off Amber's scent." It wasn't the whole reason, of course, but after the way Liz had reacted to his suggestion that they try again, he was wise enough to guess that she didn't want to deal with the whole reason just yet. "If enough people read her blog—especially if the right people read it—then they'll know that Amber is having her wedding here."

Liz ran a hand through her hair and blew out a breath. "But I still don't get why you thought you should hold my hand and kiss me."

Jason raised an eyebrow. "Was it really that bad?"

Frustration rushed forth on her face again. "You know that's not what I meant. It's just... We haven't held hands, or kissed, in ten years."

Jason had dreamed of her kisses for ten long years. But he knew that moving too fast couldn't possibly be good. Fortunately, it looked like it could be the right time for another approach entirely.

"The reason I held your hand and kissed you is because I needed to convince the reporter that I was here for myself, not Amber. You and I both know that the press doesn't need real proof of anything—just hints and suggestions—to go running with it."

"Wait a minute. You want me to pretend that I'm dating you?"

"Seems to me it's the best way to deal with the security problem right now. Because if we don't do

anything, they'll soon realize Amber is having her
wedding here."

"Whereas if we give them the impression that
we're together..."

"Then they'll soon find out that we do have a
history," he finished for her. "And if you and I give
them a show to watch—if we let them see us on
romantic dates around town—then hopefully they'll
believe that everything going on here is just about you
and me."

"We get followed by the paparazzi so that
Amber doesn't have to?" She frowned. "It actually
does make sense, but we have a lot to take care of
here, and that could get in the way of the wedding
preparations."

But Jason was afraid of far worse than that.
"Honestly, I'm not sure there will even be a wedding
if the paparazzi get hold of the truth." Amber had been
so upset by the way things had been going in France,
that another round of being stalked by photographers
might be enough for her to break.

"Okay," Liz finally agreed, "but only if Rose
and RJ also think it's a good idea. I don't want them
to get angry that I'm doing the wrong thing for their
new business."

"Well, there's only one way to find out," Jason
said, and this time he took Liz's hand simply because
he wanted to, walking back with her in the direction of
her office.

A few minutes later, he sat on the far side of
Liz's desk while she called Rose, and listened to her
explain what had happened with the reporter.

"No," Liz said. "It definitely wasn't Travis's

fault. The reporter was just really good at getting into a place where she shouldn't be. I don't think things are ruined, however, because Jason and I have come up with a solution."

Liz detailed the plan to Rose in calm, simple bullet points: It was simply what they needed to do to keep the wedding a secret. It was the best way to divert attention and give everyone at Married in Malibu the best opportunity to put together the wedding of a lifetime. Fortunately, Rose agreed that it was the best course of action.

After Liz hung up, she turned back to him. "Okay. So it looks like this is a go. What now?"

"We need to start going out on romantic dates. They have to believe we're very much in love and potentially planning our wedding at Married in Malibu. We also have to make sure that our dates take place in public places where lots of people can see us." Although he would much prefer being alone with her, he knew spending time with him in public would likely feel more comfortable for Liz. At least for their first few dates.

"I know you're right. It's just..." She sighed, but instead of saying more about the two of them, she refocused on the job they had to do. "What do you have in mind for our first '*date*'?" She put the word in air quotes as if to reinforce that it wasn't actually real.

He tried to hide how badly he wished it were as he said, "How about I make it a surprise?" He wanted some time to make sure that it would be the perfect first date after ten years of being apart.

"A surprise?" Liz had always loved surprises, but then again, his bursting back into her life had already come as a big surprise, hadn't it?

"Trust me, Liz. Please, just trust me." Though he knew it was too soon to ask her to do that, she simply nodded, then looked back at her long list while rubbing the back of her neck the way she used to when she was feeling stressed. "I know you have a lot to take care of, so I'll let you go. I'll give Amber a ring to fill her in on everything."

There were no reporters around this time when he walked out into the parking lot. For the entire drive home, he was consumed by thoughts of Liz. She had always been beautiful, intelligent, and captivating. But now, she was so much stronger and wiser. And every time they were together, she took his breath away.

When he pulled up outside his house, the blogger was waiting.

"I don't know why you're so intent on pestering me and Liz," he said, keeping up the pretense that he'd started in the Married in Malibu parking lot. "But I would appreciate it if you'd leave the two of us alone." With that, he went inside and called Amber.

"Uncle Jason, is everything going okay?"

"Actually, something has come up. A blogger appeared at the venue and when she saw me in the parking lot, she took some pictures and made some assumptions."

The horrified look on his niece's face on his computer screen was enough to let him know that he'd done the right thing by pretending to be with Liz.

"Oh no, she guessed that I'm getting married there, didn't she?" Amber sounded like she was about to burst into tears.

"Honey, it's okay. I fixed it."

"Fixed it? How could you have fixed it?"

Jason explained the situation, telling Amber about holding Liz's hand and pretending to be a couple.

"And Liz is okay with this?"

"She is," Jason assured her. "She truly does want to do whatever is necessary to make sure that you have the perfect wedding."

"That's really nice of her," Amber said. "But this isn't just about that, is it? I know you, Uncle Jason. I can see how much you care about her. You don't want this to just be fake dating, do you? You want this to be the real thing."

"Am I that obvious?"

"Only to me."

"I think I still love her," he told his niece, needing to say the words aloud to the person he was closest to. "That's the simple truth of it. I saw her again, and I realized my feelings for her had never gone away."

"Oh, Uncle Jason. I can't pretend I'm not worried about you, but I—" She sighed. "I can't believe I'm going to say this, but if you feel half as much for Liz as I do for Robert, then I think I actually understand. And I hope things work out for the two of you this time, but…"

"Don't worry, honey. We won't mess up your wedding."

"I know you would never do that. I really don't want you to get hurt again."

"I'll be careful," he promised Amber, but even as he said it, he knew that was a promise he wouldn't be able to keep. Because this wasn't about being careful. It was about so much more than that.

It was about love.

CHAPTER NINE

Only Jason could have persuaded Liz to go hiking on such a warm afternoon, especially when she had so much work to take care of back at the office. But as they made their way hand in hand to keep each other steady on the steep trail, she was so glad he had. Two waterfalls shimmered in the sunlight, and all around them the canyon was in bloom, the air perfumed with delicious fragrance.

Even better than their gorgeous surroundings? Getting to spend time with Jason again.

Neither of them had said much so far today, especially not when it was taking most of her lung power just to get up the mountain. But she loved being with Jason nonetheless, appreciated the way he noticed every bird, every flower, every brightly colored butterfly, and made sure she saw them, too.

Below them, Liz could still see the

photographers who had followed them to the hiking trail. A few hardy souls had hiked with them for a while, but as the going got rougher, they soon gave up, leaving Liz and Jason to make their way to the top of the falls alone.

When they got to the top, Jason put his arm around her. It might have been just for the benefit of the photographers' telephoto lenses, but she still felt warmed all over by his gentle strength.

"Oh my," she said as she looked at the way the hills formed a natural frame around the view and the ocean shimmered blue and serene in the distance. "It's beautiful."

"I've always thought this is one of the most beautiful views in the world."

"Really?" she asked. "After all the places you've been?"

His eyes were now on her instead of the view. "Yes, really. The most beautiful by far."

Liz knew that they were just there to put on a show. Even so, she couldn't resist putting her arms around him and holding on for a few precious moments. "Thank you. This has been wonderful. Exactly the kind of heart-pumping break I needed."

"I'm enjoying it, too, Liz. A lot."

As she drew back to look into his eyes, she wished that they could stay like this forever. But they couldn't. Not only because the others were waiting for them back at Married in Malibu to help with a hundred and one different things, but because she should know better than to walk down this road with Jason again...only to end up heartbroken once more.

Slowly, she made herself move all the way out

of his arms, then turned around and headed back down the hill toward the photographers.

* * *

"There are too many points where things aren't connecting up," Nate said, his legs tangled in wires in the alcove where he was working.

"Are you sure you should be doing this?" Margaret asked. "Liz seemed pretty insistent that you should get all the IT stuff in place before you worked on any more handyman jobs."

"Hooking up these cables is part of getting the IT stuff in place," Nate explained, then swore softly as he got a minor shock from one of the cables.

Margaret wished Travis and Daniel were there, because they were a lot better at talking Nate out of doing things that could electrocute him. But Travis was talking to the security team of one of Amber's guests, and Daniel was on the beach taking shots of the cove. Kate was elbow-deep in soil, of course, and Jenn was busy at a wholesaler's setting up an order for the wedding. Liz had left Margaret in charge, but since she was usually the one following orders, not the other way around, she honestly didn't have a clue how to redirect Nate.

Fortunately, a few minutes later, Liz came back with Jason in tow. Margaret swore all it took was Liz's confident, smiling presence for the room to seem instantly calmer.

"Thanks for keeping an eye on things, Margaret. Nathan, get out of there before you electrocute yourself—we'll get RJ to take care of that when he's done on the other side of the building. Margaret, do you still need Jason to run into town to collect Art Deco supplies for you?"

"Yes, I have a list."

Things always seemed to go faster and better when Liz was around, but, at the same time, Margaret could see that there were good reasons why Liz needed to be away, too—and not just the ones that involved keeping the wedding a secret. It was easy to see just how much Jason cared for Liz.

Actually, it was obvious that he loved her, but Margaret was just Liz's employee, and she hadn't been working for her that long, so she didn't feel it was her place to say anything. But as she went back to her office to get the list for Jason, she couldn't help but hope that everything would turn out okay—not only for Amber and Robert's wedding, but for Liz and Jason, too.

* * *

The Getty Museum had one of the most beautiful art collections in the world. People came a long way to see not only the works hanging on the walls, but the stunning building itself.

Today, as Liz and Jason walked through it, holding hands felt perfectly natural—not at all as though they were simply putting on a show for the photographers who had been outside snapping pictures of their every move.

"They have really strict restrictions on photography in here, don't they?"

"Don't worry," Jason replied, squeezing her

hand. "They're wily. They know how to pretend it's not for commercial use. I guarantee whatever pictures they take of us won't have any artwork whatsoever in the shot."

It was amazing how quickly teasing the paparazzi had become a game. A fairly fun one, actually. And as they headed over to the museum's restaurant, where they had reservations for dinner, she realized she was enjoying herself at least as much as she had on any date with Jason ten years ago. Maybe even more.

"I like to come here sometimes for inspiration," Jason told her. "For that feeling of being surrounded by the work of great artists. It reminds me that people have been doing creative work for as long as we've been on the planet and that, at one point, each of these brilliant works of art hadn't even existed yet. It's a really nice reminder that while there are always new ideas out there, the past is important, too."

Again, it felt as though he was talking about the two of them, their past and their present—and maybe even their future—colliding.

Yet again, Liz worked to remind herself to keep a safe, emotional distance. But with every second she spent in Jason's company, that reminder grew more and more difficult to heed...

* * *

For Jenn, the challenge with catering the wedding was that it wasn't just one menu—she was effectively working on five different menus at once. There was the Art Deco wedding theme, which dictated most of the layout and the decoration of the food as well as several of the dishes. There was the need to produce several different specialty menus: gluten-free, dairy-free, even sugar-free for one of the guests. And then there was her goal of using as much farm-fresh organic local fruits, vegetables, and meats as she could.

She'd been trying different dishes all day when Daniel walked in with his cameras. "Mind if I take a few shots?"

She loved having him around. Who wouldn't? Daniel was a great guy. But right now she was just stressed enough to say, "Why?"

Fortunately, he didn't seem at all taken aback by her tone. "I'd like to take more photographs for the website and the brochures. The more images potential clients see of the food, the more evocative it will be, rather than simply saying what a great chef you are."

She knew she shouldn't be defensive, especially when she hadn't made a name for herself in Malibu yet, but she still found herself saying, "I know Liz probably should have found someone with more experience, but—"

"That's not what I'm saying at all," Daniel said, cutting her off. "You're perfect." He flushed slightly before adding, "I'm just here because a picture paints a thousand words, right?"

She felt bad for jumping down his throat. She wasn't normally like this, but she was so nervous about making sure everything was perfect for the wedding. "Of course it does," she said, smiling at him. "What do you need from me?"

"Just samples of your food to photograph. In

fact, it looks like there are a dozen good things out on the counter right now, so I can get started and stay out of your way."

"You're not in my way, Daniel. You know that."

The smile he gave her lit her up from the inside out.

* * *

"How did you find this place, Jason?" They were in the middle of a beautiful Malibu spa, relaxing side by side while being expertly massaged. Liz hadn't realized just how much tension she'd built up until it started flowing out of her. "Somehow I don't see you as someone who spends a lot of time relaxing in spas."

"I'd like to think I can still surprise you," Jason said with a grin. "But the truth is that I found a promotion online for this spa. Mostly when I want to relax—or need to think—I go for a walk along the beach. But I thought with all the work you've been putting in for the wedding while also dealing with the paparazzi, you deserved a little more pampering than a walk on the beach."

It occurred to Liz that discussing the wedding in front of the two masseuses wasn't very secure. Then again, if the people at the spa did talk about it, that would only fuel the rumors about the two of them. Amazingly, the paparazzi had fallen for everything, and there were now rumors about Liz and Jason all over the Internet.

"I never thought my life would be interesting

enough to warrant attention from the tabloids. You must be even more famous than I thought," she teased.

"Actually," he replied, his gaze intense as he looked into her eyes, "I think it has more to do with the fact that you're so photogenic. If it were just pictures of me looking unkempt and writerly, they'd never print a single shot."

Even the hot rocks the masseuse arranged along Liz's spine couldn't compete with the heat of one look from Jason. And if one look could do so much, then what, she couldn't stop herself from wondering, would one kiss do?

Trying to corral her wild thoughts, she said, "I'm just amazed that so many people would take an interest in a total stranger's life."

"True," he agreed, "but at least it means we've got everything for the wedding under control."

* * *

Oh God, everything was getting out of control.

Liz had just finished reading a report from Travis about the photographers and paparazzi who had been hanging around outside the venue, hoping to see a famous face. Unfortunately, the blogger who had photographed her and Jason on that first day was proving particularly persistent. Nathan had told her about some equipment incompatibilities he needed to deal with. When Kate had come to her earlier with some suggestions for flowers, she also let Liz know that a wholesaler could have the perfect blooms on one day and that the next they could be gone. Margaret, meanwhile, needed to know exactly which flowers they were going to use so that she could pick out the perfect tablecloth to go with them.

Liz was so tempted to call Jason to suggest that they go for one of those walks along the beach that apparently did so much good for his stress levels, but how could she leave her office when there was so much to do? Especially when seeing Jason had started to feel like an addiction again—one that she couldn't stop thinking about, day and night.

"Liz?" Jenn's voice came from just outside her office. "You know how I was going to try to bake the wedding cake today? It kind of sagged...more fell apart, actually."

"It fell apart?" Liz couldn't keep a note of panic out of her voice.

"Maybe that makes it sound worse than it is," Jenn said quickly. "It's just that I've got to rebake the base, which will push back the decorations a little, and if the temperature isn't right, then there might be an issue."

"But you can do it, can't you?"

Jenn nodded. "Yes. Of course I can."

"Then I'm sure it won't be a problem." When she stepped back from her own worries for a moment, Liz understood that Jenn was simply looking for reassurance. "It's going to be fine. You're doing a great job."

It was, thankfully, exactly what Jenn needed to hear. After she hurried off in the direction of the kitchen, Liz let herself slump back into the chair. Most of the time she thrived on decision-making and planning, but right now the stress of so many details and work to be done in such a short space of time was getting to be too much. Maybe she did need to decompress a little bit after all.

And if it felt like her feelings for Jason were starting to barrel out of control as she picked up the phone and called him, she promised herself she'd only let herself be weak this one time.

CHAPTER TEN

It was hard to imagine anywhere more beautiful than the Malibu beach at sunset. Liz felt as though she were in the middle of a painting with the blue ocean in front of her, the bright yellow sand beneath her feet, and the reddening sunset overhead.

Although maybe part of the reason it seemed especially beautiful tonight was because Jason was beside her, the natural rhythm of his gait so perfectly matched to hers. And even though she knew they were holding hands for the benefit of any nearby paparazzi, she couldn't help but be struck by how natural it felt to be this close as they slowly made their way along the beach.

He hadn't said anything more about getting back together—not since that day in her office. She should be relieved. And yet, if she was being totally honest, she was more than a little disappointed by how quickly he'd given up.

"Take off your shoes," Jason suggested once they were a yard or two from where the waves lapped at the sand. He was already kicking his off. "Feeling the sand between your toes is the best way to relax."

Liz knew she should keep her shoes on to maintain at least some sort of professionalism, but how could she resist his urging to feel the sand squishing beneath her feet?

"You're right," she said after a few barefoot steps. "It really does feel better like this." Earlier, she'd been able to appreciate the beauty of the beach around her—the lapping of the waves, the calls of the seabirds, and the sounds and scents of the sea. Now she could feel the way the sand gave way beneath her feet, tiny grains falling from her skin every time she took another step.

"Just one more thing," Jason said with a smile.

Liz realized his intent a moment too late. Before she could protest, he pulled her a couple of steps sideways so that they were ankle-deep in the water. "It's cold!" she exclaimed. But both of them were laughing together as they splashed along the edge of the surf.

When the light faded, the beach air would eventually cool, but for now it was still a typically warm Malibu afternoon. Out on the water, a handful of surfers were making the most of the waves, and a few couples and families were walking along the sand, but Liz barely noticed any of them. Instead, she was totally attuned to how good it was to be with Jason—and how she wished this moment could go on forever, a perfect little bubble of happiness under the setting

Malibu sun.

"Do you want to talk about what's got you feeling stressed?" Jason asked.

"Everyone is working so hard, but sometimes it seems like we're all getting in each other's way," she admitted with a sigh. "And while I did manage to find a band who's available—a great band—it took me three hours of going through all the possibilities online and talking to a dozen managers."

"But you found them eventually," Jason pointed out. "You made it work. You've always been good at finding ways to make things work."

"Maybe," Liz said, thinking about their relationship again. Because she hadn't been able to find a way to make that work, had she? For so long, she'd wanted to believe she'd done the right thing.

But had she given up too soon?

"Definitely," Jason countered. She was amazed that he had so much confidence in her, such a strong belief that she could achieve anything. "No one else would have taken this on. And no one else would have done such a great job. Which is why I arranged a bit of a surprise for you as a way of saying thank you."

He led the way down the beach to a secluded spot hidden by the remains of an old wooden pier. There was a picnic cloth set out and a hamper on top of it.

"You arranged all of this in the time it took me to get here from the office?"

He grinned. "Actually, I was planning to do it soon anyway."

"For another one of our fake dates?"

When he frowned at the word *fake*, she

suddenly wondered if this beach picnic was meant to be more than just a thank-you or a paparazzi-fooling setup.

Was he trying to woo her again for real?

But all he said in response was, "Something like that." It certainly wasn't enough to answer any of her silent questions.

As he began to set out the picnic, Liz's heart squeezed even tighter. There were a few of the standard elements, like a bottle of champagne, but what caught Liz's attention were the herbed and toasted grilled cheese sandwiches, the hot dogs, and the muffins with chocolate sprinkles on top. How many times had they eaten exactly this when they'd been together? Not elegant food, not fancy food, just culinary experiments that had, more often than not, left them laughing in each other's arms. Laughter that had always quickly given way to breathtaking lovemaking. Heck, everything they'd done together ten years ago had led to the bedroom.

But as glorious as those moments of passion had been, she couldn't let herself forget that they'd been a big part of the problem, too. Because there hadn't been nearly enough balance between pleasure and practical. She'd learned the hard way that a foundation built primarily of desire crumbled far too easily.

If only they'd started out more like this, she found herself thinking, with romantic dates where they really got to know each other before they let passion sweep them away. Because even if they were only dating for show, the time she'd spent with Jason this past week had been absolutely wonderful.

"Do you remember?"

His voice broke her out of her thoughts. "Of course I remember," she said softly, her voice full of emotion she couldn't wipe clean. She took a bite of one of the muffins, then smiled as she added, "Who could forget our combined genius that created muffins with leftover sprinkles?"

"They're an addiction."

Liz nodded as she devoured another mouthful. "I haven't eaten a muffin with this many chocolate sprinkles in…" She trailed off for a moment before she said, "Ten years."

"It has been a long time. Too long."

It was nearly impossible for Liz not to give in to the urge to lean in and kiss him. Which meant that when a stranger intruded on their picnic, it was almost a relief to be saved from her foolish longings. It took Liz only a few moments to recognize the blogger who had forced them to start this game of cat and mouse with the paparazzi—Laurel Kingston. She wasn't on her motorcycle, although Liz had no doubt it was stashed somewhere nearby for a quick getaway.

"It's the blogger." Jason had been so calm the first time they'd run into her, yet now she could hear a thread of anger in his voice.

"Jason, it's okay."

"No, it isn't." He jumped up from the sand, and he might have been one of the action heroes from his books, given the speed with which he covered the distance between them and the reporter.

Liz followed as quickly as she could, grateful for her bare feet because her shoes would have only slowed her down in the sand.

"What do you think you're doing?" Jason said when he reached Laurel.

"What does it look like?" the woman said, snapping another shot of him and Liz. "I'm taking photos on a public beach where you don't have any security guards to take my camera."

"You think I couldn't do it?" Jason said in a low, ominous voice.

Laurel gestured to the people on the beach around them. "This time, if you grab my camera, I'll have witnesses."

"Are you really planning to just keep standing there taking photos of us having a picnic?" Liz asked.

"If I feel like it."

"And I might feel like taking your camera and throwing it into the sea," Jason growled.

"Jason, don't," Liz said as she put a hand on his arm to try to calm him down. "If you do that, it will just be giving her what she wants."

"And what do you think I want?" Laurel asked. She took another shot of Liz by way of emphasis.

"Attention, probably. A reaction, certainly. In fact, this whole thing is likely just a setup so that one of your friends can get pictures of Jason grabbing your camera and tossing it into the ocean."

The woman shook her head. "You're wrong. I don't do that sort of thing."

"You're paparazzi," Jason pointed out, making it sound like she was carrying the plague.

"I'm trying to be a serious reporter, but do you know how hard that is in this town? I won't get anywhere until I get a decent story, and Amber Blakely getting married in Malibu is a huge story."

"Except that she isn't," Liz lied.

"Everyone else might have bought you two being in love, but I have instincts and I know enough to follow them."

"No, what you know is how to follow us around and make our lives difficult." Jason's tone was hard enough to make the reporter take a step back.

"All I know is that you and Liz are treating this like it's just some big game. Besides," the woman hissed, "I've never even seen you kiss." She raised an eyebrow. "No, there's something here that isn't right."

"And you're planning to just keep following us around, intruding on our dates by taking pictures, until you find whatever it is you're looking for?"

"Well, it's a free country, and you two—I don't believe for a minute that your engagement is real. You're just acting like you're a couple to distract attention from Amber's wedding moving here from the château."

Liz could have strangled the woman, but it wouldn't have done any good. If anything, it would have only proved to the reporter that she was right.

Instead, in as calm a voice as she could manage, Liz said, "You're deluding yourself. His niece's wedding isn't going to take place at Married in Malibu. How could it, when the venue isn't even open yet?"

"And not that it's any of your business," Jason added, "but since I'm sure you already know that Liz and I were once engaged to be married many years ago..." He turned to Liz and reached for her hand before saying, "We decided we want to give the love we used to have another try."

Liz's breath caught on a gasp in her throat.

The blogger looked back and forth between them. "Prove it." She pointed at Liz. "Kiss him."

"I'm not kissing Jason in front of you just because you demand it."

"Okay," the woman said with a shrug. "Then you're just proving me right about Amber having her wedding at Married in Malibu."

"Are you kidding?" Liz's voice exploded out of her chest, far louder than she'd intended. "You're going to print a false story about his niece just because I won't kiss Jason the way you want me to?"

Laurel smiled, although it wasn't a very pleasant smile. "It wouldn't be a problem if the two of you were actually in love. I mean, if I thought you guys were for real, I'd leave you alone and find another story. But I'm not going to stand here and let you lie to me, so—"

The next thing Liz knew, Jason was pulling her into his arms and kissing her. Except that was far too simple a way of describing ten years of lost kisses rolled up together.

All the kisses the two of them might have had if they hadn't split up.

All the kisses Liz had tried so hard not to remember—and long for—while they'd been apart.

At the first touch of his lips against hers, she tensed slightly in surprise. But it didn't take long for her arms to wind around his neck...and for her to start kissing him back. Slowly at first, but then with more and more hunger as she reveled in the scent, the taste of him.

It was a long time before they pulled back

from each other, and even when she finally remembered that the reporter was still standing there, she couldn't look away from Jason's eyes.

"Wow, that was some kiss," the blogger said as she lowered her camera. She at least had the grace to bite her lip and say, "Maybe I was wrong. Seeing the two of you together like that..." She shook her head. "Sorry. I'll go and let you have your picnic."

"Good idea," Liz said, barely able to contain the triumph and the thrill in her voice, even if she was almost positive a shot of their passionate kiss would be online inside of the next hour. "I think you probably should."

Meanwhile, she still hadn't let go of Jason.

She didn't ever want to let go.

Jason couldn't stop smiling as Laurel climbed the cliff path. A few moments later, they heard the motorcycle start up and she drove away. "You were amazing. She doesn't suspect a thing anymore."

For a few minutes, Liz had completely forgotten that their relationship was supposed to be fake. But after Jason spoke about their kiss as if it was nothing more than brilliant acting on her part, she felt more foolish than ever.

Despite the ache spreading in her chest, she forced a smile as she made herself step out of his arms. "Like I said before, I'll do whatever I need to do to make sure Amber's wedding stays a secret."

CHAPTER ELEVEN

Before Liz knew it, the morning of the wedding arrived.

Married in Malibu had been absolutely transformed with gorgeous Art Deco tablecloths, furniture, and decorations. Margaret had done up the room in white and cream, with hints of red and yellow to surprise the eye. Daniel had placed multicolored filters in front of several windows, which provided a stained-glass effect throughout the room. Kate had done a wonderful job with the flowers; tiger lilies were in tall vases at the centers of the tables, while roses on long stems were artfully wound together where the bride and groom would say their vows. A local jazz quartet who specialized in reworking modern pop pieces was going through their sound check on stage. And Travis had already briefed the security people that they'd brought in.

In Jenn's kitchen, the counters were completely covered in food—which, Liz realized a beat before a wave of panic hit, was exactly how the kitchen at a wedding venue should look on the morning of a wedding. For once, Daniel wasn't in the kitchen. Instead, he was upstairs, his cameras set up to shoot each guest's arrival. Nathan was there as well, laptop at the ready, so that they could get the photos up as soon as Daniel was happy with them.

Of all of them, Daniel seemed the most relaxed. Then again, this wedding certainly couldn't compare to any of the dangerous places he'd worked in over the years. Nathan, on the other hand, looked a little jumpy, likely because he'd had far too much coffee that morning in preparation for the big event.

One by one, the cars carrying Amber's and Robert's friends and relatives arrived. Liz was extremely pleased that none of the celebrities had to fight their way through press or brave a thousand flashbulbs to get to Married in Malibu's entrance. Instead, they were able to calmly get out of the vehicles and take their time walking inside. As far as Liz was concerned, no one should have to make a hurried dash at a wedding.

"The paparazzi bought it," Liz said as she looked around at the total absence of lenses pointed at the venue. "They actually bought it."

Standing beside her with a beautiful bouquet in her arms, Kate grinned and said, "They should have, considering the effort you put in with Jason to throw them off the scent."

Effort? No, it had been a complete joy to spend so much time with Jason. More fun than she'd thought the two of them would ever have again. And if she was already sad that their game of fooling the paparazzi was through—which meant no more need for any further "dates"—she was doing her darnedest to push those feelings away.

Just the same way she'd been pushing her feelings for Jason aside for years...

As Robert pulled up in a black SUV, along with his best man, Liz reflected that ordinarily by this point, she would have met the groom many times. But the rules were obviously quite different when it came to celebrity weddings, and she was already well on her way to figuring out this new world she was working in.

She moved forward to introduce herself. "Hi, Robert. I'm Liz. I run Married in Malibu."

"Hello." He was a good-looking man, older than Amber but not enough for the age difference to be remarkable. He looked stable and dependable, not to mention perfectly at home in his wedding suit. Most of all, he looked like he was already one of the happiest men on earth—because he was going to marry the woman he loved. "Thank you for putting this together on such short notice."

"It's been our pleasure. Why don't you head inside? Our photographer, Daniel, will want to take a few pictures of you, and then we're just waiting for your lovely bride to arrive."

"I still have a hard time believing this is finally happening. With the way things were going at the chateau…"

"Fortunately," Liz said with a grin, "we were able to move faster than a French chateau." She gestured to the door again. "I don't want you to see Amber when she arrives. For good luck."

Kate led both men inside so that when Amber's car arrived a few minutes later, Liz was the only one there to greet her. She gasped as Jason helped Amber step out of the limousine. The Rose Chalet's dress designer had outdone herself with Amber's wedding dress. It was a mixture of creamy tones that made Amber's complexion come alive even better than a more classic white gown would have. She'd also been made up by a favorite makeup artist, and as a result she really did look like a movie star dream of a bride.

And...wow...did Jason clean up well. Liz had seen him in jeans so often that she had forgotten just how good he looked in a suit. She'd never forget again.

Working to cover her lapse in attention, she turned to the bride with a wide smile. "Amber, you look incredible. It's so lovely to see you again."

"Thank you for doing all this, Liz." Amber sounded overjoyed. "I really appreciate it."

"It's my pleasure. Now, are you ready?"

"Yes." There wasn't any hesitation whatsoever in Amber's voice.

Liz couldn't help but be struck by how differently she'd felt about her own upcoming wedding to Jason all those years ago. If only she'd been as confident as Amber, as mature, then maybe things—

No. It was neither the time nor the place for those kinds of thoughts.

"Let's go on through," she said as she led them

inside. "I'll leave you with Daniel to take a few quick photographs, and then we will all be waiting for you in the main hall."

Jason caught up with her as Amber paused to take pictures with Daniel. "Seriously, Liz, thank you for making it possible for my niece to have the wedding of her dreams without any reporters in sight."

"I've loved doing it," Liz told him, and she truly had—especially their 'dates.' "Now, are you all set?"

"I think so." But he looked a little overwhelmed as he said, "Although a part of me still can't believe that I'm about to give my niece away to the man she's going to spend the rest of her life with."

"I'm so happy for both of you, Jason. Truly." Her throat felt tight. "And I'll be right there for anything that either of you needs."

In the main hall, Robert was standing by the intertwined roses, waiting with obvious anticipation for his bride. Liz moved into place as the officiant, which meant that she had nearly the same view as the groom when Amber made her grand entrance—a vision in cream.

Amber's hair was loose, her veil no more than a token gesture, which let everyone see her beauty as she approached. She carried a bouquet that was almost minimalist in its simplicity, with tiger lilies forming the center of a small spray of flowers. And when Jason finally presented her to the man she was about to marry, his eyes damp as he gave her a warm hug and kissed her forehead, the look that passed between the bride and groom was one of pure, sweet love.

Liz took a calming breath, then smiled at the

happy couple and began. "We are here today to bear witness to the love between Robert Wakefield and Amber Blakely and to see them joined together in marriage. I was going to have the privilege of officiating at this ceremony, but I'm pleased to let you all know that Amber's uncle, Jason Lomax, will be marrying Amber and Robert today instead."

From the delighted gasp Amber gave as Liz stepped aside to let Jason take her place, she knew they'd done the right thing when they'd had Jason authorized as a justice of the peace earlier that week. She remained close in case she was needed, but she already knew the ceremony was going to be fine—better than fine.

Perfect.

"Amber," Jason said in his deep, resonant voice, "twenty-three years ago you completely stole my heart as a newborn baby. As your uncle, I've only ever wanted the very best for you, and I know that Robert is the man who will give you that as your husband and partner in life's adventures. Nothing but the best. And all the love in the world. Every time you two look at each other, I see so much love in your eyes. I'm beyond pleased that from today forward, you are going to be together as two halves of one whole." With each word Jason spoke, he filled up with more and more emotion, so much that he had to clear his throat to say, "Robert, do you take Amber to be your wife?"

Robert gazed at his bride in wonder. "I do."

"And Amber, do you take Robert to be your husband?"

"Oh yes," she exclaimed in a slightly

breathless voice, "I do!"

It was amazing to Liz how simple the marriage ceremony was, just a few words, a couple of signatures on a marriage license, and two people were joined together. But it was about so much more than the ceremony—it was the love between the bride and groom that truly mattered. Love that bound them together as one.

With a smile that lit up his entire face, Jason said, "By the power vested in me by the State of California, I now pronounce you husband and wife. You may kiss the bride."

Robert and Amber sealed their love with a kiss while their friends and family cheered. And as Liz watched them, she couldn't help remembering the kiss Jason had given her on the beach. One that had her constantly replaying the moment inside her head ever since.

But now was definitely not the time for daydreaming about Jason's delicious kisses...or how badly she missed them. With the ceremony over and the reception about to begin, Liz needed to be on top of her game for another few hours at the very least.

Even so, she allowed herself a sigh of relief as she watched Robert and Amber. They were so perfect together, so happy, and it meant so much to her that she'd been able to give them this precious, magical moment.

"Ladies and gentlemen," she said when the two finally drew apart, unable to take their eyes off each other. "I'd like you to join me in congratulating Amber and Robert on their marriage and in celebrating it further in the reception room just outside the double doors."

In other words, it was time for the party.

CHAPTER TWELVE

"It's amazing to think that after the work everyone here put in," Jason said, "it's over now."

He had stayed behind after the guests had gone home, the wait staff had left, and the security personnel had been debriefed, to help pick up glasses, bus the tables, and just generally make himself as useful after the wedding as he'd been during the preparations for it. At present, the others were cleaning up in other parts of the building, so Liz and Jason were the only ones on the dance floor.

"You didn't have to stay," Liz said. "You should be at home relaxing, not picking up napkins and wine glasses."

"I could be back home staring out at the ocean alone, or I could be here with you. Easy choice."

"Actually," she said, her heart racing simply from being alone with him on the empty dance floor,

"I think we're at a point where we can stop for the evening. In a couple of days the team can take down everything specific to this wedding and pack it all away in case we need to use it again in the future."

He looked around the room one more time. "I'm still amazed that you were able to create something so beautiful, just for this wedding, just for this day. And that you managed to do it in such a short space of time."

"It wasn't just me," Liz reminded him.

"No, but it wouldn't have happened without you."

Jason stepped closer then, close enough that she could smell his aftershave. Close enough to pull her gently into his arms. And even though the band had packed up and gone home an hour ago, they still swayed together on the dance floor. At least, until she corralled what little self-control she had to draw back and say, "I need to make the rounds and let the others know they should head home. I want to tell them to take tomorrow off, too, because they did such a great job."

"I'd like to thank them, too," Jason said.

One by one, they told her staff what a great job they'd done and that they should go home and get some well-deserved rest. At least, Liz hoped that was what they told the others, because by the time she got out to the parking lot with Jason, she couldn't remember half of what she'd said. Not when it was suddenly impossible to think of anything but him.

"I don't want tonight to end yet," he said in a low voice as he pulled her close. "Come back to my place."

"I don't want it to end, either," Liz whispered back. Especially because she knew that tonight might be all they had left now that there were no more games to play for the paparazzi's benefit.

As they drove the short distance to Jason's house, it was a small miracle that they didn't crash, given that he barely took his eyes off her.

"I'm so glad you agreed to do the wedding," Jason said as they pulled into his driveway.

"I'm glad I did, too. It was a great first opportunity for Married in Malibu."

"I know it was," he agreed. "But it was so much more than that, Liz."

As the weight of what he was saying—and what they were about to do—hit Liz, she knew she ought to worry about it. Ought to wonder whether being here with Jason tonight was a good idea after everything that had happened between the two of them in the past.

But right then, Liz didn't want to worry about it. Not when she was still on the high of a beautiful, romantic wedding and she didn't want to come down from it. Not now. Not tonight.

"When we were on the beach and that reporter showed up," Jason confessed, "I was so angry, because that moment was special. But then when she practically forced us to kiss—I'll be forever grateful for that."

"I will, too," Liz said with a laugh. "I almost forgot how good kissing you can be."

"How about I remind you again?"

The moment their lips met was so sweet that she sighed at the pleasure of it. Every kiss he gave her made her more and more intent on living for right now—in a beautiful present that was all about being in Jason's arms—rather than worrying about the future.

"The ocean is so beautiful tonight," she said when they pulled apart enough for her to see waves crashing outside the window.

"You're beautiful." He spun her in his arms so they were both looking out at the night together, his arms wrapped around her waist. The stars provided a carpet of glittering points that reflected off the water like diamonds.

Liz could see Jason's reflection in the window, his tie and suit jacket gone but his dress shirt still on. It wasn't his usual rumpled writer look, and it was unbelievably hot. Turning to face him again, she wound her arms around his neck and loved feeling the strength, the heat of his body pressed against hers.

Kissing her deeply, he backed her up to the edge of the table where he normally worked, and for a moment Liz thought they might not make it back to his room. Only the tumble of a stack of papers—likely important notes for his next book—reminded them of where they were.

"Maybe not here," he said.

"You're right. We'll get the plot of your next book out of order."

"I don't care about that. Just the part where anyone on the beach could see us."

Liz looked over his shoulder out the window. There didn't seem to be anyone on the beach right now, but that could change. "You're right. Not here."

"But somewhere," Jason said firmly.

Liz lost her breath at that note in his voice, one

she hadn't heard in a long time. Jason had always written heroes who were commanding, powerful, and just dominant enough to be sexy. The reason he could write them so well was that all he had to do was look in the mirror to find inspiration.

"Yes," Liz said. "Definitely somewhere."

Jason's eyes glimmered with wicked intent as he said, "It occurs to me that after a long day of working at the wedding, we could both do with a long, hot shower."

She wrinkled her nose theatrically. "Well, I wasn't going to say anything, but…"

Jason laughed and lifted her into his arms. Liz had tried to forget what it was like to have him hold her this close, how they'd been unable to keep their hands off each other, how he used to carry her off to bed and they'd both fall into it laughing. And now? Now she could so easily imagine what it was going to be like with the two of them slick with soap and tangled together under the hot water.

He carried her in the direction of the stairs, and she kicked off her shoes, slowly beginning to unbutton his shirt while he held her. He playfully pulled her fingers away, kissing them.

"Patience," he said. "After ten years, you can wait just a few moments longer."

Ten years. A part of Liz knew she should still be worried about that, about the question of how things could possibly work between them now when they hadn't worked all those years ago, back when they had been so in love and it still wasn't enough.

But right then it was easy to push all of that aside. Nothing mattered tonight except how wonderful she felt as Jason held her. Worries could wait until tomorrow.

"I think we've both been patient enough," Liz said.

And then she started to unbutton Jason's shirt once more.

CHAPTER THIRTEEN

The first thing Liz saw when she woke up was the ocean...and the first thought in her head was of Jason.

Last night had been wonderful, and even if she still didn't know what the future could possibly hold for them, she wanted to see his face again right away. Quickly putting her clothes back on, she headed downstairs, but he wasn't at his writing table, nor was he cooking breakfast for them both. Back when they'd lived together, she'd often awakened to the smell of bacon and eggs and had loved going into the kitchen to wrap her arms around his waist as he cooked. Any excuse to be close to him.

"Jason?" Liz went through the house room by room, but he was nowhere to be found. She stepped out onto the beach, but she didn't see him there, either.

"Liz." She turned to see Jason come out of the house. "Are you out here enjoying the beach?"

"I came out to look for you," Liz said, but just that quickly, she felt nervous. Nervous about what was going to happen between them on this morning after, considering that they hadn't made a single plan or come to any kind of agreement about the future before leaping into each other's arms last night.

"I'm sorry. There was something I needed to do, and I didn't want to wake you—not until I was able to surprise you with it."

"What is it?" Liz asked, her heart already beating a little unsteadily. "Have you been researching something for your book?"

"No, this doesn't have anything to do with my book."

Up until a few minutes ago, Liz had felt languid and a little bit sleepy, whereas Jason seemed to be bouncing with energy. Or, she thought as she looked at him more closely, possibly with nerves? Nerves that she couldn't help but feel in increasing measure, too.

Well, if he was worried how Liz would feel about the night they'd just shared, she could understand that, given that she still wasn't entirely sure how she felt about it. But rather than examining it too closely—and starting to freak out—she tried to remind herself that it was just one night, and one night couldn't possibly turn into a problem, could it? Especially after such a magical day.

"So where did you go?"

Jason reached into his pocket. "To get this."

As soon as he began to go down on one knee,

Liz knew what he was going to bring out. Joy speared her a beat before fear raced in to squash it. At the same time, a part of her still couldn't believe that he was actually proposing to her...not until she saw the box in his hand and he opened it to reveal the beautiful ring within, a gold band set with diamonds and sapphires.

"Jason, what are you doing?" She hadn't wanted to panic this morning, but how could she not when he was holding an engagement ring in his hand? The most beautiful ring she'd ever seen.

"I had to find this quickly," he said, still down on one knee, holding out the ring. "There was only one jeweler open so early. Fortunately, he was willing to open up his store for signed first editions."

"Jason!" Her freak-out was quickly ramping up to higher levels than she had seen in a decade. "Please—"

"Liz, will you marry me?" The words were out of Jason's mouth before she could find a way to stop them. "We've spent ten years apart, ten years that I would've loved to spend with you. The last couple of weeks have been the happiest of my life. I don't want to miss any more time with you. Not when I love you so much. I want to be with you—and not just for another week, or month, or year. Forever."

"Jason, I..." Her heart was racing, her palms sweating, her brain going around and around in dizzying circles. "I can't talk about this when you're kneeling in the sand."

With obvious reluctance, he stood, but that just ended up putting him a step too close to her. Close enough that, once again, Liz could feel the burning need for him running through her. So much dangerous desire that her thoughts zigzagged from terror to elation and back again.

"It was all supposed to be fake...these past two weeks...they weren't even supposed to be real dates!"

"It wasn't fake for me," Jason said, certainty and passion both crystal clear in his voice. "Not the dates, not the time with you getting the wedding ready, and certainly not the way I feel about you."

"But when you first came into my office, you were so angry with me."

"That's because I didn't understand why you left me ten years ago. But even that didn't change how I felt about you." He reached out with his free hand and clasped hers. "Do you think there has been a single moment in the last ten years when I haven't been completely in love with you? It wouldn't have hurt if I hadn't still loved you, but I did. I would have gone to you at any time in those ten years, if I'd thought you still wanted me."

Of course she still wanted him. There was a big part of her that simply wanted to say yes right there and then. To let him sweep her into his arms. To let him sweep every care away.

But that was exactly what had happened ten years ago—and look how that had turned out. No, she couldn't go through that kind of heartbreak and pain again. She wouldn't survive it this time.

"I can finally see that we both needed space to live our lives," he continued. "But we've had ten years. We've gone out and achieved our dreams. We're the people we always planned to be, except for one major detail—we aren't together."

Everything he said sounded perfectly reasonable. Except for one thing that he'd left out—the fact that he'd come back into her life without warning and completely turned everything topsy-turvy. Here she'd been carefully building her life for years, thinking she was a million times stronger now than she'd been at twenty-one. Only to completely lose control of herself in only two short weeks with Jason.

Liz took a deep breath. Then another when she couldn't quite get enough oxygen into her lungs. "Last night was amazing," she said slowly. "But that doesn't mean it should have happened."

"It didn't seem that way last night. I thought you were ready to be with me."

"I was swept up in the emotion of the wedding." Her voice was tight with the tears she was trying desperately to hold back. "I mean, of course I was after watching Amber say her vows."

"We both know it was more than that," Jason countered, but he finally dropped the hand holding the ring to his side.

Liz half turned away from him as she said, "How could we not get carried away when the wedding was so great? Maybe I didn't do a very good job of keeping things separated..." She wasn't sure which of them she was trying to convince more.

He put a hand on her shoulder to turn her back to face him, the contact as electric as always. "You don't mean that. I know it hasn't happened between us in what you would call a traditional way, but that doesn't mean it isn't right. I want to be with you, Liz. I want us to be together. I want us to have a home, a family."

That sounded so good, but at the same time, Liz could feel the panic rising even higher inside of her. How much of her own life would she have to sacrifice to this new future that Jason had suddenly planned for them? Would starting a family mean that he'd expect her to give up building Married in Malibu from the ground up?

"I can't," Liz said. "I just can't."

"Why not? We both have everything we want except each other."

"But it's not as simple as that," Liz insisted, her voice rising. "You're painting this scene as though it's one of your stories, as if everything just wraps up neatly because that's what the plot demands, and then everyone lives happily ever after. But real life doesn't work like that."

"Why can't it?" His question was a demand now. "Why can't we finally have our happily ever after, Liz?"

"Because this has all happened so fast that I don't even know what I really feel yet. Like it's all just what you're feeling washing over me, and I'm being swept away like driftwood into the ocean about to be carried away with the tide."

With that, she turned to walk away—no, to run—before Jason could say something that would have her losing what little self-control she had left. Before she ended up in his arms again saying yes to absolutely anything he wanted.

CHAPTER FOURTEEN

Even though Liz was the only one at Married in Malibu, it was still better than staying at home, sitting in her garden thinking about Jason, rewinding his shocking proposal over and over again in her head until she was more confused than ever. She even appreciated the hot and sweaty work of stacking and moving chairs, clearing a space in a room that was as empty as she felt. She didn't have to think in order to tidy them away—only lift and move, lift and move, lift and move.

"Hi, Liz. How are you doing this morning?"

Liz turned, surprised to see Kate in the doorway, ready for work in her gardening gloves. "I thought I gave you the day off," Liz said, forcing herself to smile even though it was the last thing she felt like doing.

"I figured there was a lot to do cleaning up,"

Kate said. "We all did, actually."

"All of you?"

One by one, each of her employees headed inside. Travis and Daniel were planning to take down some of the heavier pieces of set dressing. Jenn and Margaret wanted to remove the drapes and lighting arrangements. Daniel and Nathan intended to put the final touches on the photographs from the wedding.

Liz was amazed that they were all here. Their dedication to Married in Malibu was almost enough to reduce her to tears. Then again, the truth was that she had been on the cusp of crying ever since Jason's proposal that morning.

"Are you okay?" Kate asked a little while later as she passed with the wilted remains of some flowers from the ceremony.

"I'm fine," Liz said automatically, and fortunately Kate wasn't the type of person to press the issue.

Even so, Kate paused, looking at her with a slight frown. Thankfully, Nathan saved the day when he called out from the other side of the hall, "Liz, you're never going to believe what's happened."

His laptop was set out on one of the tables, and Margaret, Travis, Daniel, and Jenn were already gathered around it, their excitement palpable, even through the layer of gray that clung to Liz. Her team looked like they wanted to jump for joy or start dancing around the room.

"What is it, Nathan?" she asked. "And seriously, did none of you hear me when I said you didn't have to come in today?"

"You're here," Jenn pointed out.

"Besides," Margaret said, "it looks like we're going to be pretty busy."

Liz finally looked at the computer, where a selection of blogs and celebrity gossip magazines were on the screen—and every single one was reporting on Amber and Robert's wedding. None of them had photographs, but a few had quotes from the more famous guests about how wonderful the wedding had been.

Nathan pulled up one of the bigger style blogs next, big enough that Margaret gasped when she saw that Married in Malibu was featured.

"It seems that we've all been fooled, and beautifully so. Instead of marrying in a French château later this year, Amber Blakely and Robert Wakefield tied the knot yesterday in a private ceremony at a small wedding venue called Married in Malibu. No one here had heard of the venue until this morning, but judging by some of the comments from the wedding party and by how happy Amber looked as she and Robert jetted off on their honeymoon yesterday evening, we'll soon be hearing much more about it. Anywhere good enough for the happily ever after of Los Angeles's favorite celebrity couple is good enough for us." — SoCalStyle Online Magazine

"That's..." Liz was nearly speechless. "Incredible."

It was everything they could have hoped for—a perfectly private celebrity wedding followed by a big splash the next morning. If it weren't for what had happened with Jason, Liz would have been ecstatic.

But as exciting as it was, she felt the joy almost secondhand, caught behind the walls she'd thrown up to keep from breaking down. Especially when she was being congratulated for putting on happily ever afters that she still couldn't quite believe in for herself...

"You should probably let us take care of putting away the rest of the chairs," Jenn said. "It looks like the phone in your office is going to be ringing off the hook pretty soon."

"But there's still a lot of clearing up to do," Liz pointed out.

"We can handle that," Kate assured her. "But you're the only one who can book the next wedding."

As if on cue, Liz's phone began to ring. She made it to her office just in time to speak with a prominent journalist who wanted to hear more about what they did at Married in Malibu. One after another, a mixture of potential clients and interested journalists called, and somehow Liz managed to keep herself on task, rather than derailing with thoughts of Jason that lay barely beneath the surface.

When a knock came at her door, Liz was surprised to see it was late afternoon—and to find Rose Knight standing in her doorway.

"Liz, I hope you don't mind me dropping by like this." Rose's auburn hair was pulled back in a ponytail, and she was casually dressed in jeans. "Congratulations!"

For a moment, Liz froze, thinking back to Jason's proposal—but of course Rose wouldn't be talking about that, even if Liz had been thinking of little else for hours. "You mean on the wedding?"

"Of course. What did you think I meant?"

"The wedding, of course," Liz said in what she hoped was a bright tone. "I'm so glad it went well."

"Better than well. Jason called me to tell me how brilliantly it all went. He wanted to tell me how impressed Amber and Robert were with it all, too."

Jason had called Rose. What else had he said?

"You really went above and beyond, Liz," Rose continued. "And I want to say that I'm extremely proud and pleased at the way you took my dream and made it into a reality."

The first tears came then. Liz had been holding them back since the beach, but she simply couldn't do it anymore.

"Liz? Are you okay?"

"I'm fine," she replied, hoping that it would work on Rose the same way it had on Kate. But it didn't.

"Let me rephrase that," Rose said as she put an arm around Liz's shoulders. "You're not okay. Can I help?"

"I'm fine," Liz said again, but she could barely get the words out. The first racking sobs ripped through her, only made worse by her efforts to stop them and by how much she hated herself for falling apart in front of Rose. "I'm sorry. I'm…"

"Come on," Rose said, gently guiding her toward the door. "There's a coffee shop across the street, isn't there?"

Liz nodded and just barely managed to pull it together long enough for Rose to get her over to Tamara's shop. When they walked in, Liz saw the look that passed between Rose and Tamara—shared concern and the determination to help, even though the two of them likely hadn't even met yet.

Malibu T & Coffee had quickly become the place everyone on the team went to get their caffeine fix. Nate, in particular, seemed to spend almost as much time there as at the wedding venue, but Liz figured computer specialists needed coffee to run at top form.

The fact that the coffee shop was conveniently located wasn't the only reason Liz liked it. It was a homey, comfortable place with an arrangement of chairs that switched from day to day, so that one day the seat by the window might be a high-backed Georgian style but woven bamboo the next. The room caught the sun perfectly, and the coffee was so good that at rush hour it could sometimes be hard to get a seat. This being Malibu, there were plenty of tourists passing through, but it said a lot about Malibu T & Coffee that the locals kept coming back.

But the best thing wasn't the beans, the decorations, or the location. It was the owner. Tamara Truscott was tall, tanned, and wore beaded jewelry and brightly patterned scarves that made her look as if she might have just run away from a new-age community. Or was at least on her way to the beach. Tamara was friendly, intelligent, and down-to-earth, and the coffee shop had quickly become a great place for Liz to retreat to when things got stressful at work.

"Why don't the two of you sit tight," Tamara said as Rose sat the two of them down on the old-fashioned barstools at the counter, "and I'll make us all something special?" Tamara set to work with coffee...and what looked an awful lot like vanilla ice cream. "Even I don't believe that coffee cures all ills—just most of them. But today, I'm thinking we should get out the big guns and add a whole lot of ice cream to the mix."

"I'm Rose," Liz's boss said to Tamara. "And I think you're spot-on about the ice cream."

"Nice to meet you, Rose. Don't worry, I'm making enough of this sinfully good drink for all three of us," she said with a wink. "That's some great place you've got there across the street. With the best staff on the planet, if you didn't already know."

Liz was glad to have a few moments to sit back and let the whir of the blender and Rose's and Tamara's voices wash over her.

"I agree," Rose said. "I only wish we had a café like this across the street from our San Francisco wedding venue. Something tells me you must know the crew here almost as well as Liz does. I know if it were me, I'd certainly be here every day."

Tamara smiled at that before confirming Rose's guess by saying, "Margaret likes to come in before she starts work. Daniel usually drops in at the end of the day, often with Jenn. Travis is coming in more now that I've started making healthy smoothies for him. I don't actually see much of Kate, although I'm working on a new floral drink that I hope will entice her. And Liz normally breaks in midafternoon when she realizes that she's worked through lunch."

Rose raised an eyebrow. "I'm impressed."

"I don't normally spend this much time watching all my customers," Tamara said with a grin. "Only the ones I'm hopefully going to be seeing a great deal of for the foreseeable future." She slid their coffee milkshakes over, then settled in on a barstool on the other side of Liz. "First, I think you should take a long drink from your glass," she urged in a gentle voice. "And then you should get whatever is bothering you off your chest."

Rose waited until Liz had mainlined nearly half her frosty, cream-filled glass before she said, "This is about Jason, isn't it?"

Liz looked at her in surprise. "How…?"

"You told me about what used to be between you, remember? And I've seen the pictures the paparazzi has taken of the two of you during these past two weeks. It didn't look like just an act to me."

"It wasn't," Liz found herself blurting out. "And then this morning Jason asked me to marry him."

"I take it I shouldn't be saying congratulations right now?" Tamara asked.

"I panicked and I ran away. I told him I couldn't do it, that I couldn't marry him and still be me."

"I know relationships can be difficult," Rose told her, reaching out to cover Liz's hand with her own.

"How would you know? You and RJ are perfect!"

Rose laughed softly. "RJ and I definitely didn't have the perfect relationship that you think we had. For years I pushed him away. I worked with him, and I kept him at arm's length, always denying what I felt about him. I even had a fiancé I left at the altar."

"You did?" Liz couldn't believe it, not when Rose and her husband were so perfect for each other. "How? Why?"

"Because I finally realized how much I loved RJ. Fortunately, I had some wonderful people around me at the Rose Chalet who helped me see that I didn't have to push away the man I loved just to be who I thought I needed to be. They showed me that what I felt in my heart counted for more than what seemed sensible or logical or safe. And now I can't imagine what my life would be like without RJ as my husband."

The look on Rose's face as she said that—as if living without RJ was the worst thing she could possibly imagine—impacted Liz in a major way. Because the thought of never seeing Jason again...

"Now, tell me why you think you can't be with Jason," Rose said as more tears threatened to spill down Liz's cheeks.

In a halting voice, she explained how they'd started dating ten years ago and had become so close so fast that it had been utterly overwhelming—how it had felt as though her independence and her own dreams had been completely swept away.

"And now?" Tamara asked.

"I'm worrying about the same things. I'm only just getting started at Married in Malibu, and I'm terrified that being with Jason will cause the rest of my life to fade into the background. I'm scared that there won't be anything left of me if I say yes."

"You're not some twenty-one-year-old kid fresh off the bus from Kansas anymore," Rose pointed out. "You're a successful woman with everything in front of you, including the man you love, if you want him. But only if you have the courage to truly talk to him this time rather than running away again."

"It's okay to be scared," Tamara added. "We've all made mistakes when it comes to romance, but how many of us really get the opportunity to set them right? Whereas you actually got a second chance with Jason."

Liz knew they were right. She also knew what a big mistake she'd made earlier that morning. She wasn't the same person she'd been ten years ago, nor was Jason. And she shouldn't have run again. Instead, she should have trusted herself—trusted both of them—to be strong enough to actually talk things through this time.

Because even if they were both so different in so many ways, and they still had plenty of things to work out between them, one thing hadn't changed.

Love.

CHAPTER FIFTEEN

"I love him," Liz said aloud.

Looking back, it was clear that she'd always loved Jason, from the very first moment she'd met him. Even in the years he hadn't been there, her love for him had remained like an ember buried deep inside of her, waiting for him to return and bring the flames roaring back to life.

"You're saying that like it's news to us," Rose said with a smile.

Tamara nodded. "Of course you love him. The question is, what are you planning to do about that?"

Now that her eyes were finally open, Liz could see that Jason had spent the past two weeks wooing her slowly, letting her know how much he cared about her all the while. He'd spent so much time helping out for the wedding, not only because it gave them an extra pair of hands, but because it had allowed the two of them to reconnect as well.

But then, when he'd made his grand gesture on the beach, she'd run away.

Again.

"Just how hurt did Jason sound when he called you?" Liz asked Rose.

"Honestly, while I don't know him all that well, he sounded—" She paused a moment. "Destroyed."

"How well do you have to know him?" Tamara said with a shake of her head. "The guy obviously loves you to pieces, Liz. Of course he's going to be a complete wreck."

Tamara was right. Jason had offered his heart to her, along with another chance at a life together. It would take a gesture at least as grand as his proposal on the beach to undo the damage she had inflicted when she'd panicked and rejected him.

"If you truly love Jason," Tamara added, "then you should do whatever it takes to make things right."

Liz looked at Rose. "Was that what you did with RJ?"

"Yes, I ran away from my wedding to tell him how much I loved him. If I hadn't done that, I might still be with Donovan." Again, Rose's expression filled with sadness as she imagined a world where she hadn't told RJ how she felt, where she hadn't risked everything to be with him.

Liz didn't ever want to look in the mirror and see that expression staring back at her. Didn't even want to think of what her future might be like without Jason in it.

She needed to do something to prove that she

was ready to make a lifelong commitment to him. Even if their relationship wasn't always going to be easy or simple. Even if she felt overwhelmed sometimes.

Because the one thing she now knew for sure was that they definitely did bring out the best in each other. Together, they had not only put on a spectacular wedding for his niece, they'd also made each other incredibly happy at the same time.

"I have an idea that I have to try," Liz said suddenly. "Even if it doesn't work." She shook her head. "No, it has to work. Although, I might need some help."

"Whatever you need," Rose said without any hesitation, "it's yours."

"How would you like to try getting a second wedding ready in a couple of hours rather than in a couple of weeks?"

Tamara stared at her as though she'd gone mad. "I saw how much coffee you all went through to put on a wedding in two weeks. Is two hours even possible?"

Rose seemed to be wondering the same thing. "They've already torn down nearly everything in the main hall, so the time it would take to—"

"I wasn't planning on having it at Married in Malibu," Liz clarified. "I just need some help from our amazing staff. But I know you wouldn't want it to seem as if you just give your weddings away."

"From what I understand," Rose said with a twinkle in her eyes, "today is meant to be a day off for my Married in Malibu staff, and I can't control what they choose to do on their day off. If they want to help a friend with her wedding, I'm certainly not going to stop them."

"Thank you, Rose," Liz said as she impulsively threw her arms around her boss. "For everything. And thank you for the drink, Tamara." She gave the other woman a hug, too. "It turns out that a hefty dose of sugar and cream—and a good talking-to—was exactly what I needed to help me think straight."

"Anytime, Liz," Tamara said as she hugged her back. "Anytime at all."

"It's my day off, too, you know," Rose said as Liz got up to head for the door. "And I do love a good wedding."

"So do I." Tamara grinned. "And since I'm the boss here, I can take any days off I feel like. In fact, I can also take as many coffees and cakes as I'd like to cater this wedding."

Liz blinked back tears, stunned that these two women she hadn't known even a month ago had already become such good friends. As the three of them walked the short distance to Married in Malibu's main building, Liz made a quick phone call.

"Hi, Amber. It's Liz. I know it's pretty much the worst thing in the world to interrupt your honeymoon, but I desperately need to make sure that your uncle is going to be at home for the next couple of hours, and you're the only person I can count on to make that happen."

"Why do you need him at home?"

Liz took a deep breath and explained it—all of it. How hard Jason had worked for her love during the wedding preparations, what had happened that morning after his proposal, and what she planned to do now to make it right.

"You've already hurt him once, Liz. Twice. I don't want to see my uncle hurt yet again."

"Neither do I," Liz said. "I love him, Amber, and I don't want to ever hurt him again."

Amber hesitated on the other end of the line. "All right," she said at last. "I'll tell him that I want to Skype. That will keep him home."

"Thank you," Liz said. "Thank you so much."

A few moments later, as they stepped into the main hall and she looked around at her staff all working so hard, Liz realized just how well she had begun to get to know each of them—and how much she truly appreciated them all, too. She'd learned that Nathan's coffee obsession and his tendency to attempt DIY when he should be programming was a good way for his brain to let off steam when he was calculating the answer to a problem with their computer system. She'd learned Kate could spend the whole day outside in the garden if someone didn't check up on her now and again. She'd learned about Margaret's fear of speaking up in front of the others, even though her ideas were brilliant, and about Jenn's worries that things might go wrong while she was baking her mouthwatering treats. She'd learned how much Daniel adored his two children and how Travis tended to treat the rich and famous as though they were kids just waiting to get into trouble.

"I want to start by saying thank you for the work you've put in over the last couple of weeks. You've done an amazing job and now—" A part of her could hardly believe she was about to say this, but she would do anything to win Jason back. Even ask her team to pull off the impossible. "Now I need your help organizing another wedding."

"You've booked another wedding already?" Jenn asked.

Liz shook her head. "Actually, this isn't one of our official Married in Malibu weddings." She took a deep breath then told them, "It's mine."

"Your wedding?" Margaret said.

"To Jason?" Kate asked.

As soon as Liz nodded, Daniel was ready with the next big question. "How soon?"

"Today," Liz said, then watched the worry immediately appear on all their faces. "I know it seems like it can't be done. But I really hope you can help, because I just completely screwed up everything with Jason this morning." She'd never been so forthcoming with any of the colleagues at her other jobs, but this was different. The people surrounding her today weren't just colleagues. They were friends. "He asked me to marry him and instead of saying yes, I freaked out and ran. I need to fix things—I need to win him back—and I hope that he still wants to marry me."

"Since this isn't an official Married in Malibu wedding," Rose let the group know, "I'm simply here because Liz is my friend, and I want to help her."

"Where are you planning to have it?" Travis asked.

"Actually," Liz said, "I thought we'd take the wedding to Jason at his beach house."

"I have baked a few things today," Jenn said thoughtfully.

"And I could bring the leftover flowers," Kate said. "We could scatter the petals on the sand and make a bouquet from what's in bloom in the garden."

"The sunset will be the perfect backdrop for photos," Daniel noted.

"And we have enough leftover samples of material from Amber's wedding dress to make a veil," Margaret offered.

"Of course," Rose said, "I'm happy to officiate."

On the verge of tears again over how amazing her employees and boss were, Liz rushed home to shower and change into a long, white sundress—the closest thing she owned to a wedding dress. By the time she returned to Married in Malibu, the others were ready to leave, and she called Amber again to let her know they were on their way to Jason's house.

As they set off down the beach, she knew they must have looked strange, a whole wedding party walking down the sand. Travis took the lead to get them safely past people who stopped to stare—and there were more than a few who did that—including Laurel Kingston, who was heading toward Married in Malibu as though she was on a mission.

"Are you here looking for a story, Laurel?"

"After you tricked me, I came to give you both a piece of my mind."

"We had to do it for Amber," Liz said as they kept moving toward Jason's house, "but you're more than welcome to take as many pictures as you want of us today."

She'd spent so much time running away from this moment in the past that now she wanted to show

Jason that she wasn't afraid of sharing it with anyone who wanted to see. She wanted to tie herself to him as clearly and openly as she could so that he truly believed she wouldn't run ever again. If that meant Laurel and a thousand other bloggers writing pieces about this moment and running pictures of Liz and Jason together, so be it.

Silently, Liz prayed again and again that he'd accept her apology and take her back.

When Laurel fell in with the rest of them, so did plenty of other people. By the time they reached Jason's home, there must have been nearly a hundred people in the group.

Fortunately, Liz didn't have to wait long for Jason to appear on his deck. He looked every inch the jilted writer—unshaven, dressed in a T-shirt and jeans, and blinking in the sunlight as though he hadn't been outside all day. Even so, he looked amazing to Liz. He had his laptop in his hand, and Amber's face was visible on the screen.

"Liz, what are you doing here?" He spoke to her as if she were the only one on the beach, as if he didn't even see the crowd behind her. "I was just about to go find you—to beg you to forgive me for screwing up again—when Amber called and said I needed to stay home to talk with her. But then I saw you coming down the beach and—"

Forgive him? No, he had it all wrong. She was the one who needed to make things right.

Quickly stepping forward, she went down on one knee in the sand in the same spot where Jason had done so. "Jason Lomax, will you marry me?"

"You want to marry me? Here? Now?" For

once, he was the one who looked overwhelmed as he left the computer on the rail and came down the steps toward her.

"Ten years ago I loved you," she told him as she took his hands, "but I wasn't ready for a life with you, so I ran. This morning, I ran again because I realized that my love for you has grown a thousand times bigger than it ever was. But with some help from my friends, I finally realized that I'm not scared of big love anymore. The only thing I'm frightened of is living without it. Without you. And you don't have to be scared of losing me anymore, either. I'm not going to run again."

"You don't know how happy it makes me to hear you say this, Liz. But what about how I did it again? How I held on too tight? How I pushed you too hard, too fast?" He dropped to his knees in front of her and cupped her cheek with one hand. "I never meant to overwhelm you. To come on so strong that you felt like you couldn't breathe again. But I was scared. Scared that if I let you walk out of my house without my ring on your finger this morning, you'd never come back. Scared that I'd lose the love of my life all over again. I need you to know, to believe me when I say that I'm not going to make that mistake again. However much time you need, I'm going to give it to you. I promise."

As the words spilled from his lips, Liz knew without a shadow of a doubt that both of them were going to do everything they possibly could not to make the same mistakes again.

"I don't need any more time, Jason. I just need our big love. I need you."

The next thing she knew, his hands were tangled in her hair and his mouth was on hers. And this time when joy pierced her heart, there were no gray clouds anywhere in sight, no panic waiting in the wings.

When he finally let her go, she breathlessly asked, "Was that a yes?"

His grin was easily the most beautiful thing she'd ever seen as he said, "Yes."

CHAPTER SIXTEEN

The setting sun spilled over the Malibu beach in front of Jason's home, turning gold and blue to purple and red. Liz and Jason stood together at the center of a half circle formed by the crowd around them with the ocean at their backs. Rose stood a few feet in front of them to officiate. To one side, Nathan held Jason's laptop with the camera turned so that Amber and Robert would have a good view of the ceremony. All the while, Daniel was taking photographs, capturing beautiful memories that would last a lifetime. Laurel, the blogger, was also snapping away with her camera.

"By tomorrow," Jason said softly to Liz, "this is going to be all over the Internet."

"If it means I'm married to you, I want the whole world to know. Although," she added with a small smile, "a sundress isn't exactly what I'd planned to be wearing on my wedding day."

"You look perfect," Jason said, and the loving look in his eyes told her he truly meant it.

Kate had made a beautiful bouquet with roses from the garden and a few lilies from Amber's wedding, while Margaret stood off to one side holding a basket of flower petals she was planning to use as confetti. Meanwhile, Jenn and Tamara had been handing out cupcakes, pastries, and coffee to anyone who wanted them.

Even with months to plan the perfect white wedding, Liz knew she wouldn't have felt happier than she did in this moment, holding Jason's hand on the beach in front of a collection of friends and total strangers. He might not have been dressed at all for a wedding, either, but he still looked absolutely perfect to her.

"You look pretty good yourself," she told him.

"Only pretty good?" he teased.

"Actually," she whispered, "you look like forever."

Rose cleared her throat, and the crowd fell silent, a perfect hush broken only by the lapping of the waves and the calls of the seabirds. "Normally," Rose began, "I would start by talking about the friends who are gathered around the couple and about how wonderful it is to have the people they care about here with them on their wedding day. But today, even though we're doing things a little differently, the parts that matter are still here: two people who love each other very much. Not only are Liz and Jason in the presence of friends and family, but they also want to show their love to the rest of the world."

In the corporate world, there had been little time in which to build relationships. Yet, in the course of just a few weeks, Liz truly had become friends with everyone at Married in Malibu. They were the closest thing she had to family in California, while Jason had Amber and Robert with him via video link. Yet the presence of the crowd was also important today, because she wanted to shout her love for Jason to the entire world.

"I have only known Liz for a short time," Rose continued, "but I already know what a wonderful person she is, and I've seen how much of herself she'll put into the weddings she works on. Jason came to Married in Malibu for his niece's wedding, but in the process he found his own. We're all very happy that they managed to find each other again after all these years. And now I think we should hear from the two people who matter most. Liz?"

Liz hadn't written anything down, hadn't worked on her speech until it was perfect, yet she now realized that she'd been preparing for this moment for ten years.

"Jason, I loved you from the first moment we met. I never stopped loving you—not for one single second—and I never will. I want to share the rest of my life with you, and that means even more now that I have a full life to share. I love you, and I can't wait to be your wife."

"Jason?" Rose prompted in a slightly choked-up voice.

Jason took a deep breath, and it was a little strange to see someone who worked so effortlessly with words struggle to find ones that would encompass everything he felt. In the end, the words that spilled out of him were simple...and oh-so-beautiful.

"I love you, Liz. I've loved you for so long that I can't ever remember not loving you. You've been in my heart every day for ten years, even when you weren't with me physically. When I found you two weeks ago, I knew that I needed to do everything I could to bring us back together. I knew this was a second chance for both of us—not to wipe away our lives, but to make them complete at last. I can't say that I could never imagine living without you, not when we both have the memories of what that was like. But the simple truth is that my life is so much better with you, and I don't ever want to be apart from you again."

Earlier, Liz hadn't been able to cope with the intensity of what Jason felt for her, but now she realized that it perfectly matched everything she felt, too. She was more complete when she was with Jason. Better. Happier. And deeply in love.

"You have both declared your love for each other in front of everybody here," Rose said. "Now, do either of you happen to have a ring?"

"Just one second," Jason said, then ran into his house. Barely a minute later, he came sprinting back, stopping in front of Liz. He opened the box, and the slowly sinking sun caught the diamonds and sapphires on the ring. He pulled it out of the box, and as he set the ring on her finger, it felt so right.

"Liz, do you take Jason to be your husband?"

"I do," Liz said, feeling so lucky that she had been given the chance to finally say those words after all this time.

"And, Jason, do you take Liz to be your wife?"

Jason looked into Liz's eyes, and it felt like they were the only ones on the beach as he said, "I do."

"Liz, Jason, I now have the pleasure of pronouncing you husband and wife. You may kiss the bride."

Liz didn't care about all the camera flashes that went off or that there was a crowd watching. All she cared about was that she and Jason had promised their lives—and hearts—to each other.

And in that moment when their lips met, she knew that whatever the future held, if she ever ran again, it would be straight into his arms.

EPILOGUE

Two beautiful weddings in two days.

While Jason and Liz kissed to seal their vows, Jenn happily handed out the last of the pastries. She'd been worried about taking this job, fearing that it would be impossible not to be cynical about happily ever afters when her own had derailed so horribly. Yet, it felt so good to help give Liz and Jason this moment of blissful connection—even in the wake of the wreckage of Jenn's own marriage and divorce.

After Liz and Jason headed into his house, the crowd and the reporters finally started to disperse. Jenn was cleaning up the beach when a boy and girl ran up to her. They were both fair-haired and blue-eyed, the girl a little taller and older. He had remnants of frosting on his fingers, while hers were licked clean.

"Thank you for the cupcakes," the little girl

said with a big smile.

"Thank you!" the little boy echoed. He finally noticed the frosting on his fingers and started to lick them. "They were great!"

"Kayla! Adam!" Daniel was heading over to them, his camera around his neck.

Now that he was approaching the children, Jenn could see the resemblance—the same sandy-haired good looks, the same smile.

"We were just saying thank you for the cupcakes," Kayla said.

"Mmm," Adam added. "They're the best cupcakes ever."

"Of course they were," Daniel agreed. "Jenn made them. Now who wants to be in a picture?"

"I do! I do!" they both called out at once, making Daniel laugh as he lifted his camera.

Jenn had known he had children, but this was the first time she had met them. As he got ready to take the picture, she realized that if she didn't move, she'd be right in the middle of the shot with the kids on either side of her.

But when she started to step aside, Daniel said, "Stay right where you are."

"You don't want me in the middle of your photograph."

"Of course I do. You helped make this a great day, and you gave the kids cupcakes."

"The best cupcakes ever!" Adam enthused.

"They had really pretty frosting, too," Kayla added.

Jenn was glad someone had noticed. Everyone else's attention had been so focused on Liz and Jason that they had devoured the cupcakes without even looking at them.

"Those are great shots," Daniel said as he took several pictures of the three of them. "Jenn, I'm sure you've already figured this out, but Kayla and Adam are my kids."

"I'm nine," Kayla said, obviously proud of the fact. "And Adam's seven. Do you work with my dad?"

Jenn nodded. "I bake cakes for weddings."

The two children looked pretty impressed by that fact, especially Kayla. "Could you maybe come over some time and show me how to put on frosting like that?"

"I'd love to," Jenn said.

"Cool," Adam said, and with that, the kids were off and running around the beach with Daniel in laughing pursuit.

It was easy to agree to help bake cupcakes when Daniel had such great kids. Jenn loved children, and these two were very sweet. Saying yes had nothing to do with the butterflies that flew around her stomach every time she looked at Daniel. No, she couldn't afford another relationship now, not so soon after her last one had failed so spectacularly.

She wasn't ready to risk her heart again. Not yet.

Maybe not ever.

~ THE END ~

For news on upcoming books, sign up for Lucy Kevin's New Release Newsletter:

http://www.LucyKevin.net/Newsletter

ABOUT THE AUTHOR

When *New York Times* and *USA Today* bestseller Lucy Kevin released her first novel, SEATTLE GIRL, it became an instant bestseller. All of her subsequent sweet contemporary romances have been hits with readers as well, including WHEN IT'S LOVE (*A Walker Island Romance*) which debuted at #1. Having been called "One of the top writers in America" by The Washington Post, she recently launched the very romantic *Married in Malibu* series. Lucy also writes contemporary romances as Bella Andre, and her incredibly popular series about The Sullivans has produced #1 bestsellers around the world, with more than 5 million books sold so far! If not behind her computer, you can find her swimming, hiking, or laughing with her husband and two children. For a complete listing of books, as well as excerpts and contests and to connect with Lucy:

Sign up for Lucy's Newsletter:
http://eepurl.com/hUdKM
Follow Lucy on Twitter : www.twitter.com/lucykevin
Chat with Lucy on Facebook:
www.facebook.com/LucyKevinBooks
http://www.LucyKevin.com
lucykevinbooks@gmail.com

CPSIA information can be obtained
at www.ICGtesting.com
Printed in the USA
LVHW112146191022
731125LV00020B/459

9 781938 127793